"Let me go!" Joanna tried to jerk free

The movement threw them sprawling into the shallow water. "Now look what you've done!" she snapped.

"I've done nothing. It's your fault. This time you have tried me too far!"

"My fault?" Furious, Joanna ignored the lapping ocean and lashed out at him. "It was your plan to marry me to Manuel, and now it's backfired on you! If you hadn't persisted you could have stayed the recluse with your frightful scar—the *duque* who pretends to have no feelings, who denies his hot blood—"

"Recluse? No feelings? Hot blood? What do you know of it?" Rafael muttered savagely. "I could kill you." He flung her back, pinning her down in the water. Then with a muffled exclamation his mouth crushed hers in a ruthless punishing kiss that shook her soul.

WELCOME
TO THE WONDERFUL WORLD
OF *Harlequin Romances*

Interesting, informative and entertaining, each Harlequin Romance portrays an appealing and original love story. With a varied array of settings, we may lure you on an African safari, to a quaint Welsh village, or an exotic Riviera location—anywhere and everywhere that adventurous men and women fall in love.

As publishers of Harlequin Romances, we're extremely proud of our books. Since 1949, Harlequin Enterprises has built its publishing reputation on the solid base of quality and originality. Our stories are the most popular paperback romances sold in North America; every month, six new titles are released and sold at nearly every book-selling store in Canada and the United States.

A free catalogue listing all Harlequin Romances can be yours by writing to the

HARLEQUIN READER SERVICE,
(In the U.S.) 1440 South Priest Drive, Tempe, AZ 85281
(In Canada) Stratford, Ontario N5A 6W2

We sincerely hope you enjoy reading this Harlequin Romance.

Yours truly,

THE PUBLISHERS
Harlequin Romances

Duquesa by Default

by

MAURA McGIVENY

Harlequin Books

TORONTO • NEW YORK • LOS ANGELES • LONDON
AMSTERDAM • PARIS • SYDNEY • HAMBURG
STOCKHOLM • ATHENS • TOKYO • MILAN

Original hardcover edition published in 1982
by Mills & Boon Limited

ISBN 0-373-02511-4

Harlequin Romance first edition November 1982

Printed in U.S.A.

CHAPTER ONE

JOANNA quickly turned away from the man beside her and felt an uncontrollable flaming colour burn all the way from her bare toes to the roots of her bright blonde hair. She squeezed her eyes tightly shut and tried to block out the soft whisper of Roger's bathing suit as it dropped on to the sand. When his big hand gently curved across her shoulder she shuddered convulsively and bolted a short distance away from him. Her throat closed and she twisted her fingers together to keep her hands from shaking. The fear was stark in her eyes when she turned to face him.

He stood with an easy grace, his feet firmly planted in the sand, his well-muscled legs long and tanned. No white line marked where his bathing suit had been. His lithe sinewy body was tanned evenly and she was shocked that some traitorous part of her mind could admire the perfection of his lean bronze waist and hips. She jerked her fear-widened eyes to his face and resolutely kept them there. She had never seen a man naked before and she was scared to death.

'I can't, Roger!'

'What do you mean?' His deep voice was dangerously quiet.

'I—I've never——' She shook her head helplessly and swallowed.

He smiled gently, his teeth a bright white slash in his darkly tanned face. 'I know. Don't be afraid, Joanna. You haven't lived until you've experienced the freedom of swimming in the sea naked.'

She blushed even more and her eyes skittered down to his broad muscled chest before she dragged them back to his face and willed them not to stray to the tantalising display of his masculinity. 'I can't just take off my suit and join you and the others. Don't you understand? I—I've never met your friends before today. They're complete strangers. I hardly know you. I——' Her throat seemed as dry as dust, yet her mouth was filled with a salty moistness she couldn't control no matter how many times she tried to swallow.

'You've worked for me nearly two years now, Joanna. As my secretary you know more about my habits than anyone else.' His voice was cool, gently coaxing. He moved closer to her but he didn't try to touch her. 'How can you look at the Mediterranean and not want to be a part of it? The others are already in. Let's not keep them waiting. Hmm?'

She shaded her eyes and saw two other couples farther down the secluded sun-swept beach. They were without suits, swimming and splashing with an easy abandon she envied. Her fingers were icy cold as she fumbled with the thin red straps tied at the back of her neck.

'That's right.' Roger flashed a small triumphant smile. 'Here, let me help you.' His hands were warm and sure as he reached around her and expertly found the knot, all the while looking deeply into her fear-widened blue eyes. 'You look beautiful in this bikini, full of promise. Let's see if you live up to it.'

If he hadn't said anything she might have gone through with it. But he had said it and she knew she couldn't do it. She gripped his strong arms and tried to pull them away. 'No! I can't!'

Roger's eyes flared to twin flames of dusky gold fire. 'I'm getting a little tired of this display of modesty. We're all consenting adults here. You knew the score before you boarded the plane. We're on a two-week vacation in Spain and I'm not going to waste a lot of precious time trying to coax you into shedding your inhibitions.'

'But I do have them, and there's nothing I can do——'

'You can relax,' he cut in.

'I'm not one of your jet-set circle of friends. It's been fun pretending I belonged, even for just these few hours, but it's a mistake, I see that now. I don't belong. I can't go skinny-dipping with you and your friends as if it was the most normal thing in the world.'

'Good God! You make it sound positively indecent! This is a holiday. Relax—let nature take its course.'

'I shouldn't have come,' she mumbled. 'I'll go back to the house and find my own way home. Go ahead and join your friends.'

She tried to turn away from his loose hold, but he wouldn't let her go. His hands tightened at the back of her neck, drawing her closer to his tall sinewy length. 'Not so fast, Joanna. I'm not about to let you make a fool of me. I realise you're young and innocent, but there has to be a first time for everything. Just be glad that I'm the one who's going to enlighten you. I've had a lot of experience and I promise I won't hurt you.'

Her fingernails curled into the taut muscles of his arms, unconsciously drawing blood. 'Let me go!' She was sure she had shouted, but the words were a choked whisper.

'You came with me, and you're not leaving until I say so. I intended to take it slow and easy, in stages, so you wouldn't be frightened.' His lips twisted into a sneer. 'But since you prefer caveman tactics I'm more than happy to oblige.' He jerked her roughly against him and covered her mouth with his own. His hands moved low on her back, forcing her slender hips against his strong thighs.

She struggled in his grasp. She had never been this close to any man before, and certainly never near one stark naked! All that stood between them was the tiny scrap of scarlet cotton that was her bikini. He was tall and powerful, she short and insignificant. Her strength was no match for his. She would have to use her wits to get out of this. With a tremendous effort she forced herself to stand absolutely still and to ignore the flaming heat of his muscled flesh searing her pale slender figure.

Immediately he felt her capitulation and relaxed his grip on her, chuckling deep in his throat. 'That's better,' he murmured into the side of her neck before exploring its pale length with his lips. 'I can be a very good lover if you meet me half way. Your innocence intrigues me and your shyness brings out my gentler side. Don't fight me.'

Joanna took advantage of his slackened hold and kicked him on his shin before shoving at him with all her strength. Surprise knocked him off balance and he sprawled in the sand in caught-out surprise as she turned and fled silently along the sandy beach.

The fine white grains were hot against her bare feet. Her hair loosened from its confining knot and flared out behind her like a long yellow banner as she ran across the sand. The only sound that reached her ears was the painful rasping of her breath and the loud pounding of her heart drumming thick in her ears as she ran faster and faster, fear giving her a speed she didn't know she possessed. She saw the small rented cottage in the near distance, its whitewashed sides absorbing the dull flame of the Spanish sunset.

She changed her direction abruptly when it suddenly hit her that this was exactly where Roger wanted her. She was making it easy for him. In no time flat he would corner her in one of the small bedrooms and . . . Her mind balked at the thought as she plunged through a thick tangle of bushes and made her way up a rough overgrown track leading away from the sea.

How could she be so stupid? Twenty-three-year-old girls who knew nothing at all about men were unheard-of in this day and age. Yet here she was on the coast of Spain being pursued by a man she had so naïvely thought was her friend. He had been so different in the office. He kept his distance and had been kind. He never raised his voice when he corrected her errors—and there had been many when she had first come to work for him. But they gradually got used to each other, and only last week he had told her she was indispensable to him. Stupidly she convinced herself he only saw her as his efficient secretary, nothing more. This trip to Spain had been in the nature of a reward for work well done. Or so she thought.

When it dawned on her that she was to be his latest conquest, she panicked. He was thirty-five, handsome, a financial wizard and a very eligible bachelor. He could have had anybody. Why me? she wondered. And then she remembered how he had murmured that her innocence intrigued him.

She stumbled through the thick vines and plunged on, uncaring that thin branches whipped at her skin as she fled in blind panic. The air was redolent of the sea and sunshine, the heavy scent of the bright scarlet flowers scattered at her feet assailed her nose when she had to stop, gasping, and catch her breath.

She heard Roger picking his way through the underbrush and her heart stuck in her throat as she wildly searched for somewhere to hide. In her haste her toes caught on a thick root in the path and she stumbled, sprawling flat on her face on a bumpy carpet of thick green leaves.

Salty tears sprang to her eyes and she bit her lip savagely to stifle the pleading that rose to her throat when she was gently lifted from the ground. Somehow she would keep her dignity. She might lose everything else, but it would be a dignified loss. She lifted her chin and squared her shoulders and opened her eyes.

For a moment she couldn't believe what she saw. A shiver ran through her and she lifted an incredulous hand to her face. It wasn't Roger standing in front of her so still and tall and straight, it was a Spanish boy, about eighteen years old, dressed in a wrinkled white cotton shirt and baggy slacks with flashing eyes glinting black as coal. Joanna looked past him, but the vivid greenness surrounding them remained still and unbroken. Surely Roger would come crashing through the bushes any minute now and shatter this illusion.

He caught her look and spoke quietly: 'The man who was following you gave up the chase a good five minutes ago.'

His English was perfect, and then she knew she must be dreaming. Rescuers didn't just appear out of nowhere at precisely the moment they were needed. She closed her eyes and counted to ten. When she opened them again he was still there, still looking at her with a gentle smile creasing his thin dark face.

'I am not a mirage, *señorita*. I am Manuel Santiago.' He bowed slightly, regally. 'I was riding my horse up on a higher ridge when I noticed you with your friends on the beach. When you ran away I thought you might need my help.'

'Th—thank you,' she stammered, shifting from one foot to the other. There was no way she could even begin to explain the humiliating situation, so she merely smiled a small hesitant smile and remained silent.

'Do your scratches cause you pain?' he asked with genuine concern.

Joanna looked down at herself and felt a sudden warmth rush to her face. Her toes were scraped and several long scratches on her legs and arms were bleeding slightly. She folded her arms across her waist selfconsciously and lifted her chin a fraction. 'I've been stupid,' she said shortly. 'There's no excuse for it—I never should have come here.'

'You have a bruise on your cheek that requires attention. There is a first-aid box in my saddlebag. Will you come with me?'

She looked at him warily then shook her head. 'I'm not going to make a bad situation worse. Thank you anyway, but I can't just walk off with a complete stranger.' I'm trusting but not that gullible, she thought.

His smile was understanding. 'Very well, *señorita.* I shall bring the first-aid to you. If you will wait here?'

He left her standing in the path and in a short space of time he came back with a huge black stallion picking his way behind him. 'This is my horse, Saeta,' he said conversationally as he took a large box from the saddlebag. 'We travel to many out-of-the-way villages to tend to the sick.' He deftly applied antiseptic to her scratches and some sort of clear ointment to her cheek with hands that were sure and gentle.

'Are you a doctor?' she asked when he had finished.

'Thank you for the compliment, *señorita*, but no, I merely help out at the Mission. It is part of God's work too, no?'

'You're a priest?'

A wide smile lit up his face. 'You must know I am too young to be a priest.'

She tilted her head to one side and searched his face for a long moment. 'Are you being mysterious deliberately?'

'All women like a man of mystery, no?' He said it with such open charm that she was forced to return his smile. 'But alas, there is really no mystery about me. I am merely Manuel Santiago and I live a short way from here with my brother and our housekeeper. This has been my home for my entire life. It probably will be for many years to come.' A short bitter sigh escaped him, but he caught himself immediately. 'Do you wish to return to your friend now? Perhaps he has had time to—how do you say—cool down?'

Joanna bit her lip. Was she ready to face Roger again? Would she ever be ready?

'Come, *señorita.* I will go with you.' Manuel Santiago sprang to his saddle without giving her a chance to refuse and lifted her up to sit behind him. He firmly wrapped her arms across his lean waist so she wouldn't fall off and she was thankful he was in front of her so he couldn't see her blush again.

From this height she had a clear view of the now-deserted beach. 'They must have all gone to the house,' she said softly.

Manuel Santiago tugged at the reins and they made a slow smooth descent before trotting across the pale glowing sand. When they came to the beach house, now deep in shadow, Joanna felt a flicker of fear. Everything was so still and quiet.

'It looks deserted,' she said before the young Spaniard helped her dismount. She ran to the house and threw open the unlocked door and disappeared inside. The drone of an engine brought her racing back outside where she shaded her eyes with a trembling hand. The small red and white jet dipped its wings as it flew overhead and then headed towards the horizon.

'*They've gone!*' she exclaimed in a shocked, barely audible whisper. Her lower lip trembled and she bit it savagely, blinking back the tears that welled up in her eyes. 'And Roger's taken everything with him—my clothes, my purse—I have no passport, no money to get home!' She pressed both her hands to her face and tried to get a grip on herself. Panic wouldn't help anything.

'You are sure they have gone?' Manuel Santiago asked quietly.

'That was Roger's private jet. His brother flies him everywhere. They go in and out of countries like the rest of us go from city to city.' She let her breath out on a bitter sigh. Now what? She forced her chin up and faced her rescuer. 'If I went to the police, do you think they'd help me?'

He smiled admiringly. 'You do not despair, *señorita*—that is good. If you will permit me to take you to my home, my brother will know what is best to do.' He tilted his head in a faintly regal manner and shifted himself to the back of his horse. 'But this time you shall ride in the saddle, no? We have a longer distance to cover and I wish you to be more comfortable.'

'You're much too kind, *señor*.'

'Please, I am Manuel.'

'Manuel,' she said shyly. 'I am Joanna.'

It had grown quite dark by the time they neared Manuel's house which was situated on the top of a hill. Joanna could make out a wide sweeping length of green separating it from the tiny whitewashed village they were now approaching. The scent of the sea was strong and if she listened closely she could hear the whisper of the waves gently lapping the shore somewhere on her left. As they made their way up the hill she saw the house was becoming much bigger than it looked from the village. It was imposing, tall and white, looming high above the vine-covered walls of a circular courtyard. The second floor was trimmed with a delicate tracery of black wrought iron to form a balcony with tall Moorish windows shining dimly in the pale moonlight. Arched doorways led off in several different directions, she noticed with a slight shock as they passed through a black wrought iron gate opened wide to the night. They rounded a large lighted fountain set in the middle of the courtyard with water cascading musically down a black marble statue of a naked boy. A profusion of bright flowers and velvety leaves and vines spilled wildly along the stone walls dotted here and there with the soft light from strategically placed wrought iron wall sconces.

'Welcome to my home, Joanna,' Manuel said softly.

Her eyes were wide with wonder as she looked about her. 'It's beautiful!' she breathed.

'A pile of bricks and iron.' His mouth twisted, but he managed to smile quickly. 'But beautiful bricks, no?' He jumped down, but before he reached to help her from the saddle his dark eyes roamed over her questioningly. 'Before we go to my brother——' He hesitated as if not knowing what to say.

'Yes?'

'I should have told you before.' His hands were firm as he lifted her from the saddle, his voice gentle. 'I do not wish you to be hurt if he should refuse to see you. His face—is not——' Suddenly his fingers dug into her waist and she knew he didn't realise his own strength.

'What is it?' she whispered, trying to twist away from him.

'There was a time when my brother was quite handsome. Now his face is scarred.'

Her eyes widened but she didn't say anything. Manuel continued his delving scrutiny of her face. 'He was a *matador* for several years, the idol of many. Now he sits and broods. Please try not to be shocked by his ugliness.'

Joanna let out the breath she had been holding. 'I'll try not to be,' she promised.

He withdrew his hands and smiled an apology. 'Come.'

They went through an archway to a massive carved door which swung open on noiseless hinges, and Joanna's breath caught in the back of her throat when she found herself in a high-ceilinged marble hall with a magnificent winding staircase carpeted in deep red leading up to a grilled gallery. Large alabaster urns flanked the staircase and were filled with exotic flowers emitting their fragrant perfume.

Their steps were silent on the cool white marble floor. They descended two carpeted steps before coming to another heavily carved door. Manuel knocked softly before entering his brother's study. The light was dim in here and she could barely see the man who stood in the shadows.

'Come, Joanna,' Manuel said softly, squeezing her hand in gentle reassurance. 'Rafael, I have brought a guest who is in need of help.'

Soft thick carpeting muffled their steps and Joanna dug her scraped and bruised toes into its silky texture when she came to a stop in front of a huge desk.

Manuel's brother stood behind that desk in a shadowy gloom that masked his profile, and Joanna's heart pounded wildly in her throat as she imagined all sorts of mangled scar tissue criss-crossing its drunken way on his dark flesh. Were his eyes involved? she wondered. Did he have a nose? Perhaps his jaw was gone! Anyone who kept the light so dim must be horrible to look at. The blood drummed harshly in her ears and for a giddy moment she thought she might faint.

Time crawled by with agonising slowness. She felt her nerves stretched to screaming point. Still the man in the shadows did not speak.

She didn't know where she got the nerve, but she heard herself say quite clearly: 'You don't play fair, *señor*. You can see me, but I can't see you. I can only imagine what you look like!'

That seemed to break the spell that held them all motionless. She heard a slight startled gasp, but whether it came from Manuel or his brother, she couldn't tell. Suddenly the man behind the desk came right around to her and as he stepped into the circle of lamplight she saw he was an older version of Manuel but much younger than she expected. He was probably in his late twenties, she decided.

He had a long jagged scar twisting grotesquely down his left cheek from the corner of his eye to his jaw. It was roughly puckered and there were tiny holes along both sides of it where it had been stitched. The thick white line was a startling contrast to his darkly tanned complexion. He waited for her reaction, but she stared steadily back at him with no trace of the instantaneous relief she felt. A bubble of sudden hysterical laughter stopped somewhere in the middle of her chest.

With a harshness that surprised her, he glared directly into her eyes. 'Well? Shall I go back into the shadows so I no longer offend your eyes?'

Her jaw started to drop, but she quickly sank her teeth into her bottom lip. 'You don't offend me, *señor*. I imagined something much more gruesome.'

'What could be more gruesome than this?' he asked harshly.

'I—I thought you might have no eye, or that your nose was gone! Maybe even your jaw——' Her voice dwindled away in shocked stillness as he loomed close to her. He was exceptionally tall and lean and she could feel the tension vibrating from him when his face came so close to hers that she could see the length and thickness of his black eyelashes and smell the faint aroma of aftershave and tobacco smoke that clung to him.

After a moment he said something softly in rapid Spanish, then almost unwillingly threw his head back and started to laugh, a deep rumbling sound that caused her to jump in surprise. 'You have a startling imagination, *señorita.*' His dancing eyes dropped to her slim figure barely covered in the red bikini.

The slow insolent scrutiny made a flaming heat rush to her pale skin, but she stood still, in silence, and waited.

'I am Rafael Santiago,' he said in a low voice curiously reminding her of the qualities of dark velvet. He bowed with faint condescension. 'My brother has said you need our help. How may we be of service?'

She blinked and suddenly let go of Manuel's hand. She hadn't realised she was still holding it. 'I've been stranded in your country, *señor*, with only——' She looked down at herself ruefully, then lifted her chin a fraction higher than was necessary. She was practically naked, but there was absolutely nothing she could do about it. Roger had taken everything with him.

'Joanna is without means, Rafael,' Manuel said gently. 'The people she was travelling with have played a cruel joke on her and have taken all her belongings, leaving her here alone.'

She threw Manuel a grateful smile and Rafael Santiago turned slowly from his brother's bashful grin back to her to hold her gaze with a curious hauteur. Something flashed in his dancing black eyes but was instantly veiled.

'How did Manuel come to learn of your predicament?'

She twisted her hands nervously. 'I was running away—er—up a track by the sea, and I stumbled. Then—then Manuel came by and—offered to help me.' Her tongue felt tied up in knots and she knew that was really no explanation, but how could she tell a complete stranger what really happened? It was going to be bad enough trying to explain it all to the police. 'If you could help me get to a police station, *señor*, I would be very grateful.' She shivered when she thought of the ordeal ahead.

Instantly Rafael Santiago shed the dark jacket he was wearing and slipped it around her shoulders before she could say anything more. 'Manuel, will you have Josefa prepare a room for our guest? It is cool this evening and she must be tired and hungry.'

Manuel stared at him as if he couldn't believe his ears, then a sudden wide grin split his face and he almost bolted from the room.

'Oh, but that's not necessary. If you could take me to the police, that's all I ask. I couldn't impose on you like this.'

'Nonsense,' Rafael Santiago said quietly. 'It is no imposition.' He flicked on a light switch to dispel the gloom and seated himself behind his desk, gesturing for her to do the same in one of the dark brown leather chairs at its side. 'This is better than the dimness, no?'

She gave him an uncertain smile and looked at him squarely. There was a tiny sprinkling of grey glinting in his silky black hair brushing against the collar of his white silk shirt. His head was tilted upwards and there was a strong suggestion of arrogance outlining his firm jutting jaw. His nose was straight and his brows a thick black arch over flashing dark eyes that stared steadily back at her. The scar on his cheek was thick and ugly, snaking its way down his cheek, but it was not as shocking as Manuel would have had her believe.

She saw his eyes drop to the front of his jacket and automatically she pulled it closer around her, painfully aware of her near-nakedness beneath the warm smoky heaviness of the cloth. His dark brows rose and he held his head at a proud angle, staring at her, probing her face with his intent gaze. 'I am curious, *señorita*. Why were you running away from your friends?'

A huge lump lodged itself in her throat and she had difficulty in swallowing past it. 'Roger—my employer, Roger Thornton, wanted me to—go skinny-dipping with him—and his friends. I—I refused.' Two bright spots of colour stained her cheeks.

'Skinny-dipping? Why not? Surely it is an innocent thing to do?'

Her bright blue eyes darkened with humiliation and she stood up with a nervous jerk. 'That was just the beginning. He thought he'd—we'd——' She could feel another swift surge of colour rush up her neck. 'I didn't stop to think—I ran.'

'I see,' he nodded slightly. 'Did you get the bruise on your face and the scratches on your body before or after you ran?'

She blinked. 'I fell. The bushes were thick—I tried to hide.'

'It is fortunate you were not harmed,' he said softly before he arose and crossed the room with a graceful fluid motion. He stopped at a low cabinet containing a shining assortment of glasses and bottles. 'Will you join me?' His voice was gentle, soothing, coaxing as he came back with a crystal goblet cut in an intricate design in his lean fingers. 'It is wine made from grapes grown in one of Spain's finest vineyards.' He looked at her with eyes so deeply brown they were almost black. His face was dark and brooding and twisted by his scar. Try as she might, Joanna could not read his expression.

'Manuel will have taken care of his horse and should be back presently to show you to your room,' he said, sitting on the edge of his desk quite close to her. 'Tell me, what do you think of my brother?'

'He is very kind, *señor*. He has a certain ingrained courtesy that belongs only to your race.' She looked at the sparkling red liquid in her goblet and then gripped the stem with trembling fingers. She pulled the lapels of his jacket together again. It had fallen open when she took the wine from him and she didn't realise it until now. She was uncomfortably aware of the provocative picture she must make sitting in this room with his coat about her shoulders, her long slim legs gleaming whitely next to the black cloth. Fighting to control the tremors in her voice, she spoke quietly: 'If Manuel hadn't come along when he did, I don't know what I would have done.'

He eyed her thoughtfully. 'Tell me, why do you think your friends left you?'

'I'm not at all like them. They're so knowledgeable about international travel. This was just another holiday to them, somewhere to spend their leisure time, not a dream of a lifetime. I don't really know how I persuaded myself I could pretend to be like that—a real jet-setter,' she said with a choking little laugh. 'They knew it all along.'

'Because you would not remove your bikini?'

'That—and other things. I'm not used to alcohol, at least not all day long. Champagne breakfasts, liquid lunches, pre-dinner Martinis, after-dinner liqueurs——' She shook her head and swirled the wine in her goblet but did not drink it.

Rafael Santiago leaned over his desk and calmly extracted a cheroot from a long black box. He struck a match to light the tip and as the flame came close to his face, she watched his livid scar take on an even more twisted appearance. When he blew the smoke in the air above their heads she felt herself shiver.

'So you would not take off your clothes and join your friends in a little innocent fun. You could not drink with them or shed your inhibitions even though they did,' he said in a low musing tone. 'What would it take, I wonder, to make you change?' His voice was a low murmur, but she heard the words clearly enough.

She set her goblet on the desk beside her with a thump and stepped away from him. 'Manuel thought you would help me, not take up where Roger left off!' She snatched his jacket from her shoulders and stiffly held it out to him. Her face was hard and cold and full of stubborn pride. 'Thank you for the hospitality, *señor*, but I will not stay here another minute!'

He didn't take the coat from her but sat on the edge of the desk swinging one leg indolently, regarding her through narrowed eyelids. His eyes swept over her body, lingering on the soft swell of her breasts, the taut smoothness of her stomach and the white silken length of her legs. 'I am sorry if I have offended you. I did not mean to do so.' His eyes moved searchingly over her face. 'Will not your parents wonder what has happened to you?'

'No, *señor.*' She placed his coat on the desk beside him.

'No?' he mocked. 'Are you one of these liberated young women who can go all over the world and your parents do not care?'

'My parents cared about me very much and we were very close.' She lifted her chin and her eyes became deep blue with sadness.

'You speak in the past tense. Do you no longer care?'

'My father died last year from a heart attack. My mother was inconsolable. She was never very robust after we left England, but my father always hoped her health would improve. She died not long after he did.'

'I am sorry, *señorita.*' He came to stand closer to her, looking down as if from a great height. 'You are English but you do not live in England?'

'We moved to the United States when I was ten.'

He allowed a slight smile to cross his face. 'And did you miss England? Did you find it difficult to adjust to another way of life?'

'Not really. My father tried to make me see it as an adventure.'

'And this trip to Spain was also an adventure?'

'Oh no,' she breathed, 'this was a dream come true. I

was always fascinated by anything Spanish——' She stopped abruptly, realising she was telling him altogether too much about herself.

'You have no other family? There is no one who is responsible for you?'

She tilted her head to the side and frowned. 'Why do you want to know?'

His smile was bland, his eyes smooth unreadable black velvet. 'When I contact the authorities I must be able to tell them about you, Miss Joanna——?'

'Taylor,' she supplied.

'And have you a family you wish to contact, Miss Taylor?'

She looked at her toes. 'No, there's no one,' she murmured. Then she jerked her head up. 'I really must go now.'

'All in good time,' he said smoothly.

Her eyes widened. She felt herself go hot and then cold. 'Do you intend to keep me a—a prisoner here?'

His eyebrows shot up in surprise, then he chuckled. 'Ah yes, how could I forget your so vivid imagination?' His lean dark fingers slid along the jagged edge of his scar. 'Please trust me, Miss Taylor. I would not think of keeping you prisoner. I have no wish for you to stay here against your will. However, I do invite you to stay for a time as my guest.' He smiled at her wary expression. 'It would be a shame to cut your dream vacation so short, no?'

There was something not quite right about this whole thing. 'I don't trust you,' she said baldly.

He nodded, acknowledging her reluctance and gestured for her to sit down while he retreated behind his desk. 'If you stay, *señorita*, you will be doing me a great favour. Several years ago, when my wife died, Manuel became very quiet and withdrawn. I thought he would get over it in time. Then I had this unfortunate encounter with the bull.' His fingers strayed to his scar. 'Since then, this house has been—empty.' He sat quite still and kept his disturbing gaze riveted on her. 'You are the first person he has brought here in almost two years. I was intrigued to know why, and then I see that it is as simple as this: He needs to be in the company of young people again. He needs to see that there is more to life than ministering to the sick and the poor in the villages. You can make him—live again. He responds to your enthusiasm and your vivid imagination.' His smile was brilliantly white and she was fascinated by it and suddenly trapped in its spell. 'Of course,' he went on, 'you are free to leave any time you wish. But please, please, Miss Taylor, do say you will stay, even for a little while.'

She coloured at this slightly impassioned speech and tried to shake off her misgivings. 'Somehow you're turning this all around, *señor*. You're offering me a refuge, but you're making it seem as if I'm doing you the favour.'

'But you are, *señorita*, you are.' His eyes were dark and enigmatic, but he continued to smile and she couldn't begin to imagine what was going on in his mind. 'It is all very simple. Do not look for complications where there are none. Trust me.'

'I've already made one mistake today. I trusted Roger and look what happened.'

'Come, *señorita*, you are much too young to be so cynical. Fate has smiled on you. She has led you to me. I promise you you will never have cause to regret it.'

She wanted to believe him. It would be much easier to put everything in his hands, but she couldn't shake off the feeling that she would be very foolish to do so. After all, she knew nothing at all about the man except that he used to be a *matador*. He might be the biggest criminal Spain had ever known. He certainly lived in wealthy splendour isolated up here on the top of this hill. Could his wealth have been gained at the cost of many innocent lives? He might even be the head of a Spanish crime syndicate!

Rafael Santiago watched the changing expressions on her face with a slight quirk at the side of his mouth. 'Are you fond of mystery stories, Miss Taylor?'

She brushed her hair back with a nervous hand and shifted uncomfortably in her chair. 'I—yes. How did you know?'

He couldn't suppress a wide grin. 'You have a very transparent face. I am not a kidnapper nor a criminal type. I mean you no harm, believe me. The reason I have asked you to stay is exactly as I have said. Manuel could have taken you to the police or to the mission in the village or to any one of a dozen different people. Instead, he brought you here. I would like you to stay and have you get to know him. Please—trust me.'

Before she could reply Manuel tapped lightly on the door and came to stand beside her chair, beaming down at her.

'Ah, Manuel,' his brother stood and tilted his head slightly in his direction, 'Miss Taylor has reluctantly agreed to accept our hospitality and continue her holiday as our guest. Will you see to it she has everything she wishes? We must overcome her reluctance.'

'It will be a pleasure.' He gave her a boyish grin and with a flourish ushered her out of the study. When the heavy door closed behind them, Manuel took her hand and squeezed it. 'This is wonderful! Even better than I had hoped, Joanna. You have made Rafael smile again.' His dark eyes sparkled. 'Do you realise it has been nearly two years since anyone has stayed here in our house? Two years. My brother has refused to see anyone in all that time. And tonight he has asked you to stay with us. You have made him smile and even laugh again! He sees now his disfiguration could have been so much worse. I had not thought it possible you could do so much for him in such a short time.'

'But I didn't really do anything.'

'Just by being here you have done more than you know.' He kept his smile as he led her up the magnificent staircase and she welcomed the feel of cold hard iron as she gripped the intricately worked banister with a suddenly damp clammy hand.

Surely she must be dreaming? She was surrounded by luxury and kindness and Latin hospitality when she should have been roaming about the strange countryside, late at night in a bikini and bare feet, trying to explain in halting Spanish how she came to be in such a predicament. But no, the high ceilings with their dark beams were real enough, as were the ivory walls and the soft light flickering from gilded wrought iron wall lamps.

'You have a fantastic house, Manuel,' she said in a voice full of wonder when they stopped at a heavily carved wooden door.

'It has been in our family for many generations,' he replied with a trace of bitterness she couldn't understand. 'After you have bathed and changed I will show you the portraits of our noble family. It has been the custom for all the past *duques* to have their portraits painted and hung in the gallery.'

'Dukes?' she breathed, taking an involuntary step backward.

He frowned, clearly puzzled. '*Si*. Did Rafael not tell you he is a *duque*?'

Joanna stood very still. A finger of ice slithered down her spine and she rolled her eyes heavenward. 'Oh, good lord! And I thought he was a criminal. No wonder he laughed at me!'

Manuel tilted his head and searched her face. 'You

thought my brother was a criminal?' he asked in a shocked voice.

Her head guiltily bobbed up and down.

He let out a sudden whoop of delight and slapped his hand against his thigh. 'Joanna, you are priceless!' He grinned broadly and ushered her into a spacious bedroom, speaking rapidly in Spanish to the short wizened old woman who came bustling over to them.

Evidently he was telling her how stupid Joanna had been because the little woman turned shocked eyes on her. Then she obviously saw the humour of it and started to laugh helplessly. She and Manuel were doubled up with mirth, but Joanna could only stand, shifting from one foot to the other, and hope the hot colour that stained her face was not to become a permanent part of her. She had made enough social blunders in the past half hour to last a lifetime. Didn't one bow to a duke, call him Excellency and act with at least a semblance of awe and respect? Yet she had come right out and said she didn't trust him. She let him know she thought he might even be a gangster! She put her hands to her flaming face and groaned.

Tears were streaming down Manuel's face when he put his arm around her shoulder and patted her gently, choking back a laugh. 'Forgive us, Joanna. We are not laughing at you. One day you will see the funny side of all this and understand it, but for now, go with Josefa and have your bath. She has been in our family for many years and you are in good hands. I will come back when you have finished and take you down to dinner.'

Her flush deepened and her arms dropped lifelessly to her sides. How would she ever face his brother again? A Spanish duke! 'I don't think I'll ever see the humour of it,' she sighed. Then she turned and followed the little woman into the bathroom. Maybe after a good hot soak in a tub she could put things into perspective.

Once in the bathroom, however, she could only stand and gape. It was a fantastic room with mirrors on the walls and sparkling white tiles on the floor with a sunken black marble tub dominating one end of the room. Josefa liberally poured in sweet-smelling bubble bath and smiled widely, wiping her hands on a thick crimson towel.

Joanna turned to her and tried to keep the tremor from her voice. She felt so small and vulnerable in this exotic room. 'Josefa, I shouldn't even be here. I don't belong.'

Josefa dipped her head and smiled. 'You are a guest. Please undress and get into the bath. I will help you.'

Joanna backed away from her and bumped against a mirrored wall. 'I—I don't need any help, thank you.'

Josefa's face creased into worried lines. '*Señorita*, it is the customary thing. I am a servant. I always helped Doña Elena, and she never refused. Manuel has asked me to help you, to make you wish to stay here.'

'Why is it so important that I stay?'

'Don Rafael has asked you to stay, no?' Her eyes were shining with innocence.

'Oh, I see. His wish is your command.'

A small smile played about Josefa's mouth. 'Something like that, *señorita*. Now, may I help you with the bath?'

'No, thank you,' Joanna said with a little toss of her head. 'I've been taking baths by myself since I was five years old.'

'Very well, I will go, but when you have finished I will come back to brush out your hair.' Josefa reached out and touched the bright blonde mass. 'I have never seen hair of such a colour. It is beautiful, *señorita*. When I comb it, I will make it even more beautiful, yes?'

Joanna sighed. 'All right, Josefa. Come back in a little while when I'm done.'

When the servant left, closing the door softly behind

her, Joanna quickly stepped out of her bathing suit and into the bath. It was a bit tricky because she had never before had an occasion to bathe in a sunken tub, but she settled herself in the scented water and allowed herself a moment to wonder what Roger would say if he could see her now.

It was a sheer stroke of good fortune for Manuel to have been riding by when he did. She couldn't help wondering if Roger had seen him and that was why he hadn't followed her up the track. She had to admit Manuel made a dashing figure on the back of his huge black horse. A little like El Cid, she thought, then laughed at herself.

She had seen that movie half a dozen times and her parents overlooked her childish infatuation for the famous medieval knight in chain mail wielding his broadsword. She knew it was absurd, but that had been the beginning of her fascination with Spain. She had told them one day she would fall in love with a man like that and she would ride away into the sunset on the back of his white horse. She had been eleven at the time.

She sighed and closed her eyes and leaned back in the tub, letting the hot water soothe her bruises. She had been very young then, but now she was a grown woman and she was here in Spain where lots of men looked like El Cid. She pictured Manuel, and all at once his face was superimposed by a more forceful dark handsomeness. In a few years Manuel would look like his brother. She could already see the same arrogant tilt to his black head. And the way he had hauled her up into his saddle! Her romantic heart fluttered.

The Duke must have been overwhelmingly attractive before his face was altered in the bullring. Women must have thrown themselves at his feet, but he would not deign to notice them. Not a man of his arrogant stature. Not until—what was the name Josefa had said?—Doña Elena.

That was it. She couldn't help wondering what his wife was like. She must have been a woman of spirit to be married to a duke who was also a *matador*.

'*Señorita*, are you finished?' Josefa stuck her head around the door.

'Just give me another few minutes,' she said frantically, sliding down deeper into the water.

Josefa stepped into the room and picked up the bikini from the floor. 'I have something else for you to wear when you have finished. I will wait outside the door.' She smiled slightly at Joanna's blush and quickly disappeared.

When she stepped from the bath she quickly huddled into the warm red towels and walked back to the bedroom somewhat apprehensively. It was a spacious room, much bigger than any she had ever seen before and she felt very much out of place. At one end was a wide bed covered with a gold silk bedspread that shimmered in the soft lamplight. A long fitted wardrobe with ivory louvred doors ran along one wall and a low rosewood dressing table with a wide mirror seemed to take up most of another. The carpet was thick and deep and her toes curled into the soft ivory pile. Gold and ivory damask curtains billowed out in the breeze from the long windows, and she shivered.

Josefa was nowhere about, but she saw a shimmer of black on the bed and walked quickly to it. Josefa was kind to loan her one of her dresses, she thought. Most likely it would be a very poor fit because the woman was much wider than herself and she would feel ridiculous in it, but not half so ridiculous as when she had stood in front of a Spanish duke in just that tiny red bikini.

She put a hand to her throat and gasped when she looked down at a black silk dressing gown. It was long and sleek and smelled of aftershave and tobacco smoke!

Joanna pulled the towel tighter around her slim body just as Josefa came back. 'I am sorry, *señorita*, I have put your bathing suit to soak and it took a little longer than I expected.' She did not look one bit contrite and Joanna thought she detected a hint of a devilish smile playing about her carefully blank face.

'You don't really expect me to wear that?' Joanna pointed to the dressing gown.

'It will be too big, but it will cover you.'

'Do you know what I'd look like?' she whispered, horrified.

Josefa rolled her eyes. 'You were almost naked in that bathing suit and you did not mind. There are only men in this household and they understand.'

'But I wore the bathing suit on the beach so I didn't feel out of place until I got here. In this,' she shuddered when she picked up the black silk, 'I'd look so much worse!'

'If you do not get out of those wet towels, you will catch cold, *señorita*. Please?' Josefa smiled sweetly and walked to the dressing table. 'Come and sit. I will brush your hair.'

She had no choice in the matter. There was no getting through to the woman, so she stifled a sigh of frustration and slipped on the gown, tying it tightly around her waist, trying to ignore the sensuous feel of the material as it hugged her skin. Its width was nearly doubled and the sleeves came way past her hands, making her look lost and vulnerable.

'It is only for tonight, *señorita*,' Josefa said, and Joanna thought she could detect an air of repressed excitement about her. 'Manuel will have something else for you tomorrow. You look very nice.' She helped to roll up the sleeves and then took the towel from her head. 'Such beautiful hair! I have never seen such a colour. Is it real?'

'Yes,' Joanna sighed. 'I don't dye it, if that's what you mean.'

The woman's wrinkled face smiled into the mirror as she deftly lifted a gold-backed brush and gently began to brush the silky hair. The long smooth strokes were curiously soothing and Joanna felt herself beginning to relax.

'That is right, *señorita.* Doña Elena always said this was the best way to relax.'

'It must be very lonely for you, Josefa. From the way you speak of her, I gather she was your friend as well as your mistress?'

'Friend?' Her eyebrows descended into a bitter frown. 'I do not think she is the type to call anyone friend, not even Don Rafael. Why do you ask?'

'Oh, I just wondered. When—Don Rafael spoke of his wife, he seemed sad.'

'His wife? He spoke of Doña Matilda?'

'Doña Matilda? I thought you said her name was Elena?'

'Bah! He would not marry such a one as she!'

'Oh?' Joanna looked puzzled. 'Who was she, then?'

Josefa's face drew into a stern cold frown. 'She came to teach us English and lived here many months. She was very beautiful but very cold and haughty. I knew she did not really love Don Rafael, even though she tried to make him believe it. It was his title she loved. When he was close to death after his last *corrida*, I know she came to him and told him she could not bear to stay here and look at his face.'

Joanna's breath caught in her throat. 'But that's terrible! His scar isn't that bad. How could she say such a thing?'

'Some women can be very selfish.' She stopped brushing her hair and rested both her hands on Joanna's shoulders, looking at her in the mirror. 'If Don Rafael had died, she would have been a wealthy widow, not his *duquesa*. That is all she cared about—being a *duquesa*. But I can see you are altogether different. You have a kind heart and you would not wish to hurt Don Rafael. Manuel was right—you will be good for him.'

Joanna stiffened, staring at her for a full minute before letting out her breath on a ragged sigh. 'I don't know what you and Manuel have planned, but whatever it is, there's no way I can help. I don't know anything about your customs or your way of life. Don Rafael extended an invitation to continue with my holiday here and *that's all*.'

The little woman returned an exaggerated surprised look at her. 'I have phrased it badly, *señorita*. There is nothing Manuel and I are trying to do.' A tell-tale flush crept into her cheeks, but she said no more and merely wound the golden mass of hair about her hands and wrists and swung it into a twisted knot at the nape of Joanna's long white neck. 'This is the perfect hairstyle for you, *señorita*. It shows off your milky white skin.'

She was inserting the hairpins when a soft knock on the door brought Manuel back into the room. He had showered and changed into a pair of dark brown slacks that were tight-waisted and emphasised his lean build. His shirt was buff-coloured silk and rippled over his broad shoulders in the soft light.

'You look lovely, Joanna,' he grinned at her reflection in the mirror.

She shot him a look of exasperation. 'We all know very well what I look like dressed up in your brother's robe. This is absurd, Manuel. There must be something else I can wear? One of Josefa's dresses?'

'Anything I have will not fit you half so well.'

'Josefa is right. You are decently covered in this dressing gown and I am sure Rafael will not object that I have loaned it to you. It is not so becoming on him.' He and

Josefa exchanged a conspiratorial smile.

'There's no getting through to either of you, is there?'

Manuel raised his eyebrows in mock innocence but said nothing.

'If I can see that you're up to something surely your brother will too,' she said very softly.

A fleeting look passed between Manuel and Josefa before he bowed deeply and extended his arm to her. '*Señorita*, will you come with me to the *sala* for an *aperitivo* before dinner?' He tried to sweep away all her reluctance with a bland innocent grin that didn't fool her in the least.

With a feeling of helpless inevitability she left the room on shaking legs. They had nearly reached the bottom of the staircase when Joanna thought she would give it one more try. 'I don't think your brother is going to like this at all, Manuel. Have you thought about what he might have to say?'

'You worry too much, Joanna.' He put a reassuring hand over hers resting in the crook of his arm and smiled directly into her eyes. 'Your eyes are like deep blue sapphires. Did anyone ever tell you that?'

She stamped her bare foot on a thickly carpeted stair and glared at him. 'It won't work, Manuel. Whatever it is, it won't work.' She tried to release one hand from his while clutching at the gaping front of the black silk robe with the other, but Manuel had a much stronger grip.

'Do not be angry with me, Joanna. You are very lovely and I know you can help my brother. You are a beautiful girl and he needs to see that you find him attractive. His scars are not repulsive and he will no longer need to hide in the shadows.'

'Oh, stop it! You're going about it all wrong!' She continued to struggle with him and finally he released her and she fell back against the steps. 'You're trying to throw me at your brother without any regard for my feelings—or his. Do you think he'll thank you for that?'

Manuel hung his head. 'I am sorry, *señorita*, if you think I am using you. I only want to make him happy again. If you could have known him before! He has changed so much in the last two years.'

She stood up and put a hand on his arm, her expression veering between irritation and sympathy. 'I know you mean well, but don't you see, you're going about it all wrong!'

'No.' He gripped her shoulders desperately, pulling her close to his lean body, and she struggled against the increasing pressure of his fingers.

'Well, well, what have we here?' The massive front door swung shut behind the tall forbidding figure of Rafael Santiago. He leaned negligently against it and eyed them both with mocking laughter.

But Joanna saw an expression in his eyes that made her feel as if she had just been struck. Her startled gaze was unwillingly drawn from his twisted, sneering lips to the powerful muscles that jerked beneath his white shirt. He flicked his riding crop against one high leather boot and quirked an eyebrow at Manuel who stood rigid with embarrassment.

'I have just come in from a very refreshing gallop across the shore and what do I find? My brother and our guest grappling on the stairway.' Heavy sarcasm dripped from his voice.

Instantly Manuel's arms fell stiffly to his sides.

Joanna's jaw dropped and she snatched her hand away from him with a terrible flush of guilt rushing to her face.

'So you are a man, after all, Manuel!' said Rafael with undisguised contempt.

Joanna's breath caught at the back of her throat as she looked away from both of them. 'It would be better for everyone concerned if I didn't stay here,' she muttered.

'No, please, Joanna.' Manuel's dark eyes were pleading.

'You cannot leave here, *señorita*,' his brother thundered, straightening from the door and staring at her coldly. 'Must I remind you, you have nothing in the way of a passport? I am sure the police would not feel very well disposed towards you in that—attire. If you try to explain your position, I do not think they would believe a word you said.' His flashing dark eyes swiftly travelled from the top of her head to her toes sticking out from beneath the front of his robe. They were full of amused mockery, but his lips thinned into a tight straight line and she was uncomfortably reminded that she did not have a stitch of clothing on underneath the black silk.

She clutched the front of the robe together and glanced desperately at Manuel, but he had withdrawn into himself and hung his head and said nothing.

Should she throw herself at this arrogant duke's feet and beg for mercy? she wondered hysterically. If she thought she had troubles when Roger abandoned her, they were nothing compared to this! Almost unconsciously she squared her shoulders and tilted her chin a fraction. 'I seem to be caught between a rock and a hard place, *señor*. At least you could have the decency to tell me what you want of me.'

A glint of unwilling admiration for her courage to say such a thing to him came and went in his eyes and he nodded in silent acknowledgement. 'I have requested your so charming company for a few weeks, *señorita*. Nothing more, nothing less,' he said in a curiously gentle voice that made her feel like crying. He walked across the hall to her and reached out, deftly removing the pins from her hair. Immediately the thick gold mass spilled down her back in shining disorder. His fingers seemed to cling to it for a fleeting moment, but she must have only imagined it, for he stepped away from her at once, his hand held stiffly at his side, his face curiously grim. 'Now you look like Joanna,' he said huskily, and looked straight into her startled eyes.

Her heart lurched crazily and stuck in her throat. She marvelled at the way his eyes burned through her with a piercing blue-black fire that somehow attracted even while it repelled. Dragging her eyes away from his, she encountered the livid white streak that slashed an angry crooked line down his cheek and she barely suppressed a shiver of reaction.

He did not miss her look and immediately a shutter closed over his expression. His lean fingers lightly traced the puckered edge of the ugly scar. 'This has been an unfortunate misunderstanding, Miss Taylor. Manuel should have chosen something more suitable and less provocative for you to wear this evening. I am sure if he had stretched his imagination in another direction he could have found something else.' He shot his brother a derisive glance. 'Tomorrow when you go to the shops to find something for our guest, I hope your discretion is allowed full rein. Try to find something that would meet with your Tia Isabel's approval.'

A doubtful smile played about Manuel's face. 'But Rafael, you know Tia Isabel disapproves of everything connected with us.'

'Try, little brother, try.' His eyes flickered over Joanna's figure again. 'With the right clothes even Tia Isabel would approve of her.' Sudden amusement danced in his eyes. 'Can you imagine her reaction, Manuel?'

He looked at his brother and then back to the pale still girl beside him. 'No, Rafael, I do not think she will be at all pleased.'

They both chuckled with satisfaction as if amused by

some schoolboy prank they were about to play on an unsuspecting aunt.

She looked worriedly from one to the other but said nothing.

'Do not look so worried, *chica*,' Rafael swept a gracious bow before her. 'You are under my protection. I shall not give you any cause to ever regret that action.'

She felt a terrible sense of foreboding. Rafael Santiago was a handsome, forceful man and he must have been irresistible before he had been gored by a bull. His smile was dazzling, but she couldn't help feeling that, however unwillingly, she had put herself in the hands of the devil himself.

CHAPTER TWO

LOOKING back on that evening, Joanna was amazed she was able to live through it. The formal dining room with its massive table and heavy chairs, the gleaming silver and crystal and china winking in the candlelight, the muted light from the heavy iron wall sconces casting shadows on huge old portraits all served to remind her that she sat in the presence of Spanish royalty.

Rafael Santiago sat at the head of the table with Joanna at his right and Manuel across from her. She tried to force herself to assume a position that could pass for composure, but found it extremely difficult to try to eat a meal with one hand while clutching at the gaping front of Don Rafael's robe with the other.

Several times she caught his wry smile and each time she coloured painfully. She was sure he was laughing at her. With each glance he seemed to be assessing her and as the minutes passed, she became more and more convinced that she was woefully lacking in his estimation.

Manuel smiled reassuringly throughout the unusually long meal but that only served to increase her nervousness.

'Will you have more wine, *señorita*?' Don Rafael said, reaching for the bottle of red table wine that accompanied the meal. 'There are times when it helps to steady the nerves.'

She didn't really want any more, but she didn't know how to refuse gracefully. Already she'd had more to drink than she'd ever had at home. 'Thank you, Your——' she stopped abruptly and swallowed. Should she call him 'Your Excellency'? After all the other things she said this evening, it seemed ludicrous. She wished there was some way to start all over again but on the right foot this time.

Don Rafael finished filling her glass and became very still. His black brows rose slightly at her apparent hesitancy. 'Is something troubling you?'

She looked at him and tried not to be intimidated by his alert watchfulness. Everything he did reminded her that he was a duke who was once a brave *matador*, undaunted by public opinion and fearless in front of a ferocious bull. If only his tie was on crooked or his shirt wrinkled or his dinner jacket crushed, she thought, then she would feel he was at least human. But he was the image of perfection. Not a hair was out of place. Only the long disfiguring scar marred his face. But to her it made him no less handsome. There was a striking vitality about him, an aura of virility and a touch of hauteur. He sat tall and straight and still and stared at her with a relentless unnerving scrutiny making her shudder.

'Manuel told me you're a duke!' she blurted out.

His lips twisted. 'Yes, that is correct.'

'Am I supposed to call you "Your Excellency"?'

He lifted his chin and his eyes hardened to icy black coals. 'If you wish to overlook the fact that I have a title, I will not be offended.'

'I never met a duke before, you see, and—and I wasn't sure if you expected me to call you "Excellency" or "Your Grace" or——' her voice trailed off miserably.

'In Spain a man is usually called "Don" followed by his first name. I believe it is comparable to the word "mister" in your country. I am Don Rafael Luis Eduardo Santiago y Bivar, Duque de las Ventas, and several other titles that go on and on. But it is much less formal merely to say "Don Rafael".' A flicker of amusement crossed his face as he leaned forward closer to her. 'Tell me, does my being a *duque* make any difference to you?'

For an instant, while he waited for her answer, she thought she could detect a flash of pain in his eyes, but it was gone so quickly that perhaps she only imagined it. She blinked several times but never took her eyes away from his. He would never know how difficult it was to fight the sensation of panic rising in her throat. 'As long as it doesn't bother you, then I won't let it bother me either,' she said in a breathless whisper.

Something snapped inside him, releasing the tension that was heavy in the room. He stood and bowed deeply to Joanna and nodded to Manuel. 'Please excuse me,' he said quietly. 'I have many things to attend to. I will be in my study, if you will ask Josefa to bring my coffee there?' Firm unhurried strides carried him silently from the room.

He was barely out the door when Manuel wadded up his napkin and bolted around the table. 'You are wonderful, Joanna!'

'Wonderful?' She couldn't believe her ears. 'Why on earth would you say that?'

He put a gentle hand on her shoulder. 'You did not let

my brother intimidate you. He is a nobleman able to trace his ancestors back to the eleventh century, but you did not let that impress you in the least.'

'And that makes me wonderful? I don't understand you at all.' She ran a dazed hand across her eyes feeling a little sick. 'In all truthfulness, I probably hurt his feelings. I actually told him it didn't matter to me that he's a duke!'

'Does it matter?'

'It must! Don't you see? Here I am, sitting at his table sharing a meal as if I belonged. If you could see the apartment I rent in New York City, you'd know just how out of place I am. I have two rooms with a gorgeous view of a brick wall. The kind of people you are, the life you live, it's like something out of my wildest dreams. You're aristocracy, Manuel! I'm just ordinary.'

He looked at her with a puzzled little smile. 'I am ordinary too. It is my brother who is the *duque*. If he dies without having a son to pass on his title, I will inherit it, and that is something I do not wish to do. So many people stand in awe of Rafael because of his title, not because of the man he is. I would not like to have people think of me as different from them just because of something I have inherited. That is why it is good you told Rafael you did not mind him being a *duque*! You were able to stand up to him.' His face took on a soft, faraway look. 'Like Matilda did,' he whispered. 'My brother greatly admired that quality in her.'

Joanna stood up with a jerk and the room rocked beneath her feet. She put a hand to her head and felt herself swaying. 'Please, Manuel! I'm sure I'm nothing like Matilda. You mustn't try to put me in her place.'

'Is that what you think?'

She nodded faintly.

'Is it that obvious?'

'Yes.'

An impish grin split his face. 'Well then, I will have to be more subtle, yes?'

'No!' she said in exasperation. A sudden nausea welled up in her throat and she pressed her trembling hands to her face.

Instantly Manuel gripped her elbow with gentle concern, noting her sudden pallor. 'You are ill?' he said softly.

Her breath came in great gulps as the room spun sickeningly, tilting in the strangest way. 'It's the wine, I think.'

'Permit me to help you to your room. If you lie down, you will feel better.'

She looked up at him, blinking as his face danced before her eyes. If only he would stand still so she could look at him! And then she was standing outside the door of her bedroom wondering how she got there. She blinked again. 'Thank you, Manuel,' she murmured. 'I'm sure I'll be all right now.'

'If you need anything, my room is down the hall. Try to sleep and do not let anything trouble you. Things will look differently in the morning.'

She watched him retreat down the hallway and silently let herself in the bedroom. A few more seconds and she would have been sick all over him, she thought, as she ran, retching, to the bathroom.

Joanna slept badly and it was late the next morning when she stirred in the wide bed. She blinked rapidly at the gold and ivory curtains moving in the faint breeze coming from the open windows and for a moment she wondered where she was. The gentle sound of waves lapping at the shore in the far distance filled the spacious room as her eyes travelled curiously from the long windows to the high wide bed she occupied.

Abruptly all the events of yesterday came back in full force to her consciousness when she spotted the black silk robe at the foot of the bed. How could she forget, even for a minute, how sick she had been? When she finally finished in the bathroom last night, she had taken off Don Rafael's robe and climbed between the sheets without bothering to feel the least bit concerned that she had no nightdress. That had been the least of her worries.

She had tossed and turned but could not relax. She punched her pillow and wanted to cry, but the tears would not come. She was numb and exhausted, bewildered and a little afraid. It was unforgivable of Roger to go off and leave her stranded like this. And it was absolute madness to stay in this house with a powerful duke and pretend she was having a wonderful time. This country was strange to her; their customs were not hers. She couldn't even handle the most innocuous table wine the way they did.

'What must they think of me?' she had moaned into her pillow. Then exhaustion claimed her and she slept dreamlessly.

As she pulled the sheet closely around her, a sudden rush of mortification overwhelmed her again. She had never slept without clothes before. She had never been sick from drinking too much and she had never felt so alone and abandoned as she did now.

Her hands clenched on the sheet as she slid from the bed. Pushing open the long windows, she looked out. The sun was high overhead and the deep green of the valley with the tiny whitewashed village nestling at its base was below her, and she sighed at the feast of beauty that was hers for the taking. She was here in the land of her dreams with all the exotic breathtaking splendour she imagined it would possess. If only I could have come here under different circumstances, she thought to herself, I would be so thrilled.

Sighing deeply, she turned back to the magnificent bedroom and stopped short, peering cautiously at several boxes that were piled on an ivory damask chair in a far corner. She didn't remember them being there last night.

When she lifted off the cover of one box, she caught her breath delightedly. A dress of the finest blue silk lay within the folds of white tissue paper. She quickly opened the other boxes and found, to her surprise, that Manuel had forgotten nothing. There was sheer lacy underwear and a delicate lace slip that must have cost the earth. He even remembered fine nylon tights and a pair of white low-heeled sandals.

She quickly gathered the things together and went into the bathroom. Barely ten minutes later she emerged feeling infinitely better after a stinging hot shower. Manuel had been right when he said things would look differently in the morning. She was hardly able to contain the excited bubble of happiness that rose inside her when she slipped the blue dress over her head. Its gossamer folds clung to her slender figure as if it had been made especially for her. The square neckline, short sleeves and slightly flared skirt enhanced her fragile bones, and as she gazed at herself in the mirror, she couldn't believe this was Joanna Taylor staring back at her. It gave her a great measure of confidence to be dressed this way, and for a moment she preened like a peacock. Never before had she owned a dress quite like this one.

Then suddenly she remembered who she was and how she came to be here. These clothes would cost her at least a full month's salary, and she bit her lip worriedly. How was she ever going to pay for these beautiful things?

She straightened the bed quickly, out of habit, then made her way down the wide curving stairs with some trepidation. Finding no one about in the hushed silence, she walked along a sunny, many-windowed hallway hoping to find the kitchen.

'*Buenos dias*, Miss Taylor,' Don Rafael spoke quietly behind her.

She jerked violently and turned towards him.

'I am sorry if I startled you.'

'I didn't hear you coming,' she said with a funny little catch in her voice. She pushed the golden wisps of her hair away from her face and looked up at him.

He was dressed all in black and looked taller and leaner this morning. He carried a book in his hand and his black shirt was open at the throat, revealing dark curling hair on his broad chest. With the bright sunlight playing over his face, his scar was even more cruelly pronounced. His openly admiring gaze disconcerted her as his dark velvet eyes travelled slowly and deliberately over her figure. When he looked again at her face, lingering on the pale blue shadows under her eyes, his own eyes narrowed.

'*Muchas gracias*, Don Rafael,' she murmured, hating the betraying colour that rushed to her face. The confidence she had found only moments ago suddenly fled.

He gave her a look that made her quiver. 'This is amazing, something I never thought to see! You are trying to speak our language even though you told me you do not know it.'

'I only know a few phrases. If this trip hadn't been such a spur-of-the-moment idea, I would have taken a crash course in Spanish conversation.'

He shook his head slowly. 'A woman who does not rely on everyone else speaking her language,' he mused. 'You are unique.'

She broke her gaze away from his, hating the cynicism of his statement. 'The clothes are lovely, Don Rafael,' she said.

'Do you like them? Everything is the correct size?'

'Oh yes. I'm amazed that Manuel could choose each size so perfectly and I admire his taste. But——' She bit her lip. Her hands were clasped in front of her and she struggled to maintain a calm front, but it became more and more difficult as he stood with such unnerving stillness in front of her, watching so silently.

'But?' he quirked an eyebrow.

She took a deep breath. 'I don't know how I'm going to pay you for them. I think they must be terribly expensive.' Her skin turned a bright red under his narrowing scrutiny but she had to make him understand that she had her pride too. She lifted her chin and looked directly into his strangely shimmering black eyes. 'When I get home—if you will allow me to send you a little money each month——'

'Enough!' he thundered, the quick flare of his temper lashing at her like the stinging flick of a whip. His face was as hard and cold and inflexible as steel. 'Do not speak of it again. It is an insult to me.'

Without thinking, she put her hand on his sleeve, feeling the taut muscles ripple beneath her trembling fingers. 'I didn't mean to insult you but it's very difficult for me to be an object of anyone's charity.'

His command of English evaporated as he began to mutter rapidly in Spanish, his voice full of cold fury. His eyes became glittering slits that bored through her. 'Never consider it charity!' he said in a heavily mangled accent.

A shiver ran down her spine at the nearness of his proud face set in hard uncompromising lines, his eyes blazing with that strange blue-black fire. He looked as if he actually hated her at that moment.

Suddenly some devil inside her came to life and she became quite calm. He wasn't the only one who had his pride. She would never buckle under to his hateful strength and haughty arrogance. Manuel said his brother admired those who would stand up to him. That was what she would do.

'Very well, Excellency,' she bowed facetiously and moved her hand away from his arm.

'Do not ever call me that!' His fingers bit into her wrist, jerking her so that she fell against him.

'Then don't you call me Miss Taylor any more,' she said without flinching.

He looked slightly taken aback. She was sure no one ever dared talk back to him, and the knowledge that she could disconcert so haughty a man, even for a moment, gave her a fleeting sense of elation.

'As you wish—Joanna!' Her name on his lips in a slightly husky murmur successfully shattered her composure into a thousand slivered fragments. His fingers stopped biting into her flesh and began a slow seductive trail up her arm, sending shock waves of awareness to all her tingling nerve ends. His face was so close to her that she could see the strong beat of his heart pulsing in his neck, the hard angle of his jaw disfigured by his scar, and the firm line of sensuality across his lips.

Her head pounded violently, making her shudder as the floor began to sway in dizzy circles. 'Rafael,' she whispered ever so softly.

Instantly he stiffened and stepped away from her. A closed, guarded look moved over his face. Like a glacier, she thought. And he deliberately traced the cleaving path of his scar across his cheek, watching her reaction dispassionately as his lean sensitive fingers lightly bumped over the ugly puckered seam. It was as if he would not allow himself—or her—to forget the cruel result of his faulty judgement in the bullring. But why? Why did he have to draw her attention to it? Surely he had forgotten it, just as she had, when he looked at her so deeply only a moment ago.

'Did you wish something from the library, Joanna?' His voice was cold and once again he had command of himself.

She looked nonplussed and then, to her annoyance, a hot wash of colour began to creep up her neck.

'That is where this hallway leads,' he said drily.

'Oh.' She gathered her scattered wits with difficulty. 'Actually I was lost. I was looking for Josefa.'

'The kitchen is this way,' he drawled, leading her towards another corridor. 'This house is large, but you will soon get used to it. Manuel will show you around in time. But now you must have something to eat.' He pointed to the kitchen door. 'Most likely you will find both my brother and Josefa in there—cooking up something.' He smiled a wry wintry smile and left her.

Manuel and Josefa were seated at a large round table in the middle of the sunny kitchen deep in conversation, and both looked up guiltily when she walked across the dark red tiles towards them.

'Joanna!' Instantly Manuel was on his feet. 'You look beautiful this morning.' He gripped her hands and scanned her figure, beaming down at her. 'The blue of the dress does match your eyes, just as Rafael said it would.'

'Si,' Josefa chimed in, 'you look lovely, *señorita*. Your skin is like ivory—and such blue eyes and such gold hair!' She stepped closer and smiled, touching the soft waves that framed her face. 'But you should wear it up, yes?'

Joanna looked doubtful, suddenly remembering the way Don Rafael had pulled the pins from her hair last evening.

'Our climate is much warmer than yours,' Manuel added hastily, throwing Josefa a curious warning look. 'It would probably be more comfortable for you to wear it up. I am sure that is what she means.' He tried very hard to look innocent.

'Come and sit down, *señorita.*' Josefa bustled her towards the table, not giving her time to dwell on it. 'Will you have coffee and a roll first? I would have brought you something to your room, but Don Rafael said to let you sleep this morning.'

Joanna glanced at the clock above the great black range with its collection of pots bubbling merrily. 'Good heavens! It's eleven o'clock already. I never sleep that late.'

Manuel gave her a conspiratorial wink. 'I hope you slept well. Some people find that our wine relaxes them so much they sleep through anything.'

She coloured painfully. 'And I did find your wine relaxing, didn't I?'

He chuckled. 'That is what I like about you, Joanna. I knew you could laugh at yourself.'

She smiled ruefully and sat at the table, accepting a cup of coffee from Josefa. 'I didn't feel much like laughing last night, but you were right when you said things would look different in the morning. I don't even have the headache I expected to have.'

'I am so glad.' He sat down next to her. 'Did all the clothes fit you? Rafael was sure they would, but I was not so positive.'

Her cup clattered on the saucer. 'Your brother gave you my sizes?'

'He did not have to. He changed his mind about me choosing your clothes after all. When the shops opened this morning, he telephoned and told them specifically what he thought you would need. His taste is *esquisito*, no?'

'Oh, Manuel!' she gulped. 'I just met him in the hallway and told him I admire your taste. I thought you chose them!'

'Ah. Now he knows you were sincere in your compliment and not just humouring him.' He grinned broadly and rubbed his hands together, inordinately pleased about something. 'I overheard him on the telephone this morning,' he said softly. 'He told the shopkeeper he wanted a dress of the finest material in the colour of a summer sky to match a beautiful woman's eyes. As for your undergarments——'

'Please, Manuel!' She put her hands to her burning cheeks. Somehow she didn't want to hear what he might have said. There was something so intimate about a man buying a woman's clothing and suddenly she couldn't bear it. She pushed her coffee away and stood up with a jerk.

'What is wrong, Joanna?'

'Nothing. I—I'm just not hungry this morning.' Her appetite fled with the sudden thought of that dark brooding duke somewhere on the other side of the house who knew enough about women to accurately guess her correct size even down to her bra. The clothes seemed to burn her skin and she shivered.

'You really should eat something even though you do not feel hungry now,' Manuel said, ignoring her look of distress. 'We will be out most of the day, and the restaurants in Malaga do not serve half so good a meal as Josefa does.'

'What?' She lifted a dazed hand to her face.

'Rafael has given me a list of all the other things he wishes you to have, but he thought you would prefer to choose them yourself when we go out today.' He reached in the pocket of his navy blue slacks and pulled out a folded piece of paper and handed it to her.

She couldn't read the bold Spanish handwriting, but the list looked exceptionally long. 'But this must be a whole wardrobe! I can't possibly let him buy so many things! I won't be here long enough to wear them.'

'If you let him hear you say anything like that, I am afraid he will take it as an insult,' he said quietly.

'I already have!' she almost wailed.

'Oh, Joanna, you should be happy he is doing this. Because you are here and in need of our help, he is taking an interest in things outside this house for the first time in two years.' His eyes roamed over her face with an eager intensity. 'Matilda always enjoyed it when he bought her clothes.'

She glared at him. 'I'm not Matilda! I told you that before.'

Manuel's carefully blank, innocent expression troubled her. She had the sensation that Don Rafael was right, his brother was cooking up something.

A little while later, full of misgivings, Joanna waited in the circular courtyard while Manuel went to get the car from the garages. She gazed idly at the beautiful fountain and tried to let the gentle murmur of the splashing water soothe her.

Soft, cat-like footsteps on the ground made her stiffen. This time she heard Don Rafael coming and was prepared for his soft voice directly behind her. When he spoke she didn't even flinch.

'I trust you will have a pleasant day with my brother?'

She turned and looked up with a hesitant smile. 'How can I even begin to thank you?'

'It is I who should thank you.' He bowed graciously. 'You are giving Manuel back to me.'

A ghost of a frown crossed her face. 'I don't know what you mean.'

'Manuel was always a happy eager child, always full of life. It has not been easy for him these last several years.'

His hand strayed to his face, but halted before he reached the scar. He turned away from her, looking at the riot of flowers spilling down the far wall of the courtyard. 'Already he has been transformed overnight. He smiles so much now. He is eager to live again because you are here.' He turned and looked at her strangely and bowed his dark head again. 'He will enjoy taking you to the shops for the clothing you will need. You will not deny him this pleasure?'

What he was saying was so much like an echo of Manuel's words, it was uncanny. Joanna gulped awkwardly. 'But surely you don't have to spend a small fortune on me——' She quailed at the hard look he threw her.

'I am a wealthy man. If I could not afford to be generous, I would not do so. Believe me, I would do anything to keep——' He bit back his words abruptly and turned away as if regretting his outburst.

Just then Manuel drew a sleek black car level with the lacy wrought iron gates that stood open at the entrance to the courtyard. He quickly stepped around to the passenger door with a small crest on the side and bowed gallantly.

'I feel like Cinderella, off to the ball,' Joanna murmured.

'Let us hope the car does not ride like a pumpkin,' Don Rafael nodded in a faintly condescending manner before disappearing back into the house.

As they settled back in plush leather seats, Manuel set the car in motion and pulled away from the gates. 'Did Rafael tell you to oversee my driving?' he asked. 'I saw him talking to you when I drove up.'

'You mean keep an eye on you? No. Why do you ask? Are you such a terrible driver?'

His teeth were starkly white in his dark face as he grinned at her. 'It is the truth that I am more at home on the back of a horse than behind a wheel. Usually I walk to the village when we need something, but today I thought we would drive into Malaga. The shops there are bigger and have a better selection for you. We will take the coastal road—the drive is scenic and you will see parts of my country that ordinary tourists miss. That is all right with you?'

'Whatever you say, Manuel.' Joanne forced a laugh and tried to relax against the seat as the shiny car silently wound its way down the hillside. It would have been so much better if they were merely on a sightseeing trip rather than a shopping expedition, but on a lovely day like this she would not let anything trouble her. She was in Spain. She would enjoy herself in spite of the handsome scarred Duke who 'would do anything to keep——' What? she wondered.

Her troubling thoughts became dim echoes as she absorbed herself in the surrounding countryside. The whisper of the sea dulled her apprehension as it floated in through the open windows of the car. How beautiful and soothing was this land with its bright sun and wide expanse of lush green hills. In the near distance was a village and Joanna glimpsed a tall white spire through the trees.

'Is that a church, Manuel?' She leaned forward and pointed through the windshield.

'*Si*. That is the Catholic church, Our Lady of Mercy. It is many centuries old.' He glanced away from the road long enough to see the eager curiosity on her face. 'Long ago the villagers were simply people who paid their respects to the naiad of the freshwater spring there. When the Catholic Church first came to this country, they discovered they could not prevent this pagan custom from flourishing, so instead of forbidding the reverence for the place and gaining the wrath of the peasants, they merely changed the dryad into the Virgin Mary and renamed the spring the Fountain of Our Lady of Mercy. That is why you will find countless Christian shrines at these springs in Andalusia.'

Joanna laughed delightedly. 'Spanish people must be the essence of tact!'

'We have our moments,' he grinned.

As they neared the village, she was entranced by the small houses crowding each other on the narrow dusty streets. They were starkly whitewashed and crowded with bright pots of trailing vines on the windowsills. Several streets led off to the right and left and small signs with arrows pointing in different directions were tacked on a pole near a large stone well.

But all at once she noticed how the whole village looked strangely deserted. Why weren't children playing in the streets and dogs and cats running loose? Then she caught sight of a woman ducking into a doorway on the outskirts and she looked questioningly at Manuel as they drove by.

'Did that woman run and hide?'

He shrugged his shoulders. 'She is shy, perhaps. This car is easily recognisable, even if it has been a year since my brother has come this far.'

Her puzzled eyes met his squarely. 'Is everyone hiding? Why is no one about?'

'This is normally time for *siesta*, which is still observed here. The sun is hot and the few shops that are here are closed in so small a village.'

'Oh, I forgot.' Then the rest of what he said implanted itself on her mind. 'You say your brother has not come this far in a year? Yet this village is close enough to your home for you to walk here!'

'*Si*. He does not venture away from our house except at night when the darkness can hide his face, and then he only rides his horses along the shore, alone.'

'But that's absurd! That scar isn't so terrible that he

should cut himself off from people that way. Are you sure that's what's made him do it? A mere scar?'

'Rafael does not think it is so small a matter. He is very conscious of the disfiguration. Almost a year ago he came here and a young girl came upon him in the street. I can still hear her terrible shriek.' He shuddered. 'It was very cruel and wounded him far more deeply than the bull did. That is why it will take another woman to make him see that she was wrong. He is not ugly. He is not an affront to anyone's eyes!' Manuel gripped the steering wheel until his knuckles were white and stepped on the pedal with a heavy foot as the car shot forward, leaving a trail of dust behind them.

'If it bothers him that much, why doesn't he have plastic surgery?'

'Once he did plan to have surgery on some of the scars on his back and chest, but then he refused to alter them. One time when he had been drinking quite heavily to ease the pain, he told me those scars would always serve to remind him never to trust a woman. He had been guilty of a very grave mistake and he would let nothing make him forget it. He loved her, and she betrayed that love when he needed her most.'

For the better part of an hour the countryside flashed by in a hazy green and blue blur while they unconsciously broke all speed limits. It was a good thing no one was on this little used road, she thought grimly, because Manuel just might end up getting them both killed. He certainly had a fierce protective pride where his brother was concerned.

'We are almost there, Joanna,' Manuel said suddenly. 'See?'

Her first sensation upon reaching the city of Malaga was one of disappointment. She knew comparatively little about the geography of Spain, having unconsciously weaved her daydreams about its people and its climate on an historical level. Now she was confronted with the more contemporary mundane matters of its business and commerce. This was a bustling seaport with traffic-congested streets, modern hotels and crowded office buildings. Harried businessmen with attaché cases rubbed shoulders with all kinds of tourists filling the pavements, and it surprised and disappointed her. Her dreams of El Cid had no place in all this hustle and bustle.

Manuel found a pleasant side street and parked the car with a minimum of fuss in spite of the amount of traffic flowing past. His eyes were warmly sympathetic when he turned to her. 'I sense you are disappointed, Joanna,' he said softly, giving her an irrepressible grin, 'but you will feel better after you not only see the city but also feel it.'

She smiled back selfconsciously. 'I just didn't expect it to be so modern.'

'No?' he sounded shocked. 'But how can this be? When you came here, did you not pass through a modern airport?'

'No. Roger's brother knew of a private landing strip. He said it would save a lot of unnecessary Customs delays.' Her eyes widened. 'I think it was against the law, wasn't it?'

'It was very much against the law. Your friend could be in very big trouble.'

'He's no friend of mine, and it took this trip to find out just what a snake in the grass Roger could be. I never want to see him again! When I get home, I'm going to have to find another job.' She pressed her hands to her face in remembered humiliation, but Manuel captured them in both of his.

'Would you consider staying here indefinitely and making Spain your home?'

Her eyes widened. 'That's impossible!'

'Why? You said you must look for a new job. You could find one here in my country.'

'This is just a holiday, Manuel. I've got to go back.'

'Rafael told me you have no family. And now you say you have no job. Perhaps there is some man waiting back home for you?'

She shook her head. 'No, no one. I suppose you find that strange? I'm twenty-three and I haven't even got a boy-friend.'

'Not at all,' he grinned, opening the car door with a flourish. 'I find it fascinating. But you do wish to marry one day and even raise a family?'

'Yes, some day,' she sighed wistfully, thinking again of El Cid. 'But I don't think the man of my dreams is on the too near horizon.'

'You never can tell,' he said with a wide grin. 'Sometimes when we least expect it . . .' He snapped his fingers like a magician. 'You are a romantic, Joanna, perfect for the Spanish way of life. Now let me show you how delightful modern Spain can be.'

His enthusiasm was infectious and her tireless energy matched his for most of the afternoon as they went from shop to shop, looking at everything they had to offer. At first Manuel thrust dress after dress at her, insisting that each of the brightly-coloured gypsy costumes was just right for her, but she resisted his impulsive selections, preferring more muted colours to the gaudy ruffled brightness he liked.

'I don't mean to be so choosy, Manuel, but I know what I like.' She took the blazing red and black satin form-fitting dress from him and held it up to the front of her. 'And this definitely isn't it.' She put it back on the rack and smiled politely at the dark little saleslady hovering behind them.

So far she had found only one white cotton sundress

with delicate embroidered flowers along the square neck. Manuel didn't seem pleased, but he cheerfully paid an exorbitant amount for it and insisted on a large white straw hat with gaudy straw flowers to complement it.

'You will need it to protect your so pale skin from the sun,' he grinned.

Joanna accepted after much haggling with him over the price, and he promptly put it on her head as they walked from the shop.

'This is unreal,' she murmured, gazing past the congested traffic to the crowded sidewalk cafés across the street. 'The scents, the heat, the noise!'

Manuel laughed. 'It has been said that to the Spaniard, happiness and noise are only different words for the same thing. But come, you must be getting tired. We will go to a little inn I know for a quiet relaxing meal. Maybe if you eat something, you will feel more able to choose clothes.'

He steered her off the main thoroughfare and they found themselves in a much quieter section of the town with a cooler breeze blowing in from the sea. They walked up shallow white steps to a low sprawling building surrounded by tubs of flowers.

'This is not like the government-owned *paradores*,' he said, shrugging into the black sports coat he carried over his arm. 'They are much more magnificent, but this place has a charm of its own.' He pulled a dark red tie from his pocket and knotted it perfectly while they were being led to a quiet table for two near a window with a gorgeous view of the sea.

'Sometimes I think you're a magician,' Joanna laughed, and hid her hat on the floor next to her feet. 'Imagine finding a quiet place in this city and then being dressed for it too!'

'One must be properly dressed for *comida* with a beautiful woman,' he said with all seriousness. Then a grin split his face when he whispered: 'Wait until you see the waiter's face when I order a hot dog and a Coke.'

Her lips twitched. 'To each his own, I suppose. Would you mind if I tried one of your Spanish dishes instead?'

'But of course. Would you like me to recommend something? Their *Malagueña* soup is out of this world and the grilled red mullet is superb.'

'That sounds fine with me. But please, no wine with it. I'll have coffee instead.'

He grinned and placed their order with a certain suavity, and she had to keep her face towards the windows so as not to give in to a fit of laughter.

Many severe looks were cast in their direction by dark-skinned businessmen dining in the room, but they ignored their silent censure and enjoyed a delicious leisurely meal of hot dogs and seafood in the quiet elegant graciousness of the seaside inn.

When they had finished eating, she refused dessert and sat back, sighing contentedly. 'That was delicious, Manuel.'

'Do not tell Josefa that. You will hurt her feelings.'

Just then a young man in jeans and a wrinkled sports coat strolled past their table, stopped, stared at Joanna, and after a moment he shook his head and went on his way.

'It must be your hair and your fair colouring,' Manuel said, grinning. 'It is good to know that I am the envy of every man here.'

Joanna blushed delicately. 'You certainly can turn on the charm, can't you?' she teased.

Several times after that the same thing happened. A man would stop suddenly, stare hard at her and then shake his head, smile politely as if he had made a mistake, and then walk on. It was beginning to make her nervous and she frowned questioningly across the table to Manuel.

'Excuse me while I pay our bill,' he said. 'The ladies' room is over there if you care to use it.' He pointed and then left her.

When she returned to their table a few minutes later, he was standing with a newspaper tightly folded under his arm, his face colourless, a worried frown along his brow.

'We must leave at once, Joanna,' he said abruptly.

'What is it?'

'Please do not ask me. We must return to Rafael.' With a hand under her elbow, he urged her through the glass doors, past a comfortably furnished parlour and out into the waning sunshine. She almost stumbled in her haste to keep up with him.

'Did something happen?'

He unceremoniously pulled her through the narrow streets after him. 'My brother will know what to do,' was all he would say.

When they reached the car, he unlocked the door, threw the box containing her sundress into the back seat and barely gave her time to gather the blue folds of her dress around her when he slammed the door.

'Oh, Manuel, I forgot my hat in the inn,' she said, her eyes wide and frightened in her flushed face. 'You rushed me out of there so fast I forgot to pick it up.'

'It is of no matter,' he said distractedly as he reversed the car from the parking space and joined the traffic leaving the city.

He had thrust the newspaper on the floor beneath his feet and she stared at it, feeling the mounting tension in the confines of the car. 'There's something in the newspaper that's upset you, hasn't it? Won't you tell me, Manuel?'

'I cannot,' he said through his teeth. 'We must go to Rafael.'

The countryside flashed by in a blur as they sped back to his home. What could possibly be so wrong that he couldn't talk about it? A dozen different possibilities flashed through her mind, but in the end she had to discard them all and merely wait until they reached his home. This had nothing to do with her.

She looked at Manuel's grim profile as he steered the car around the rutted roads of the village. His face was white and pinched. He held himself as stiff as a tightly coiled spring. Twice they had to wait while a farmer cleared his stray sheep from the road. He gripped the wheel and muttered something in Spanish that took no knowledge of the language to understand.

'Whatever it is that's so wrong, Manuel,' Joanna's voice shook, 'I hope it won't be too disastrous for you.'

It was nearly dusk when they stopped at the iron gates. Don Rafael was waiting in the courtyard, and one look at his rigid stance and deliberate expressionless face told her that he, too, must have seen the terrible news in the evening paper. He looked questioningly at his brother and received an imperceptible negative shake of his head. 'Please come to my study,' he said with deadly quiet, and went into the house.

Joanna turned away. Whatever this disaster, she wished she could help. But what could she do? When it came right down to it, they were strangers to her and she'd probably just be in the way.

Manuel touched her elbow. 'Come, Joanna.'

'Is there something, anything, I can do?'

He looked at her numbly. 'Rafael is waiting for us.'

'Us?'

He blinked rapidly and gripped her elbow. *'Si.'*

She took a deep breath to steady herself. 'Has this

something to do with *me*?' Her eyes were suddenly round with fear. 'Is there something about *me* in the paper? Is that why those people stared at me in the inn?' Her heart began to pound madly and there was a dull roaring in her ears. The thought had not occurred to her before now. 'Tell me, Manuel!'

'Joanna!' Don Rafael had come back to the doorway. 'I am waiting for you.'

On shaking legs she followed his straight uncompromising back to the study and nearly collapsed into a chair in front of the desk. All this time she was wishing she could be of some help to Manuel and Don Rafael too in their time of trouble but now they were here, helping her. 'What is it?' she whispered.

A glass was pushed into her hand and she glanced dazedly at the cold hardness of it against her shaking fingers.

'There has been an accident, Joanna,' Don Rafael said quietly. 'A small jet crashed in the Sierra Nevada east of here yesterday evening.'

Her face drained of colour and she looked at Manuel.

'*Si*. A small red and white jet,' he said softly.

'Roger's plane!' she whispered through stiff lips, standing up with jerky wooden movements, setting the glass on the desk.

Don Rafael took it and wrapped her fingers around it, firmly covering them with his own before lifting the glass to her lips and forcing her to take a deep drink. She choked and coughed before he would take the glass away. His voice was quiet: 'Five people were found dead, Joanna. No one could have survived the crash. It is most likely they died instantly. But a handbag was thrown clear of the wreckage and not burned with some of the other luggage—your handbag, Joanna, with your passport photograph in it.'

Manuel opened the front page of the newspaper and held it before her stricken gaze. 'Here is your picture. The authorities are asking for any information as to your whereabouts. They have checked with the local police and are combing the mountains for you.'

She had the distinct feeling she was losing contact with everything about her and her eyes blurred. 'They think I was on the plane? That somehow I survived when all the others died?' Then she started to moan hysterically. 'Of course—I should have been with them. If Roger hadn't been upset with me, I would have been killed too!' Tears streamed down her face as Don Rafael's tall body wavered in front of her watery gaze.

His vivid dark eyes were intent but not cold, his lips full, not thin with grimness. When she looked directly into his face, she didn't see the disfiguring scar, the ugly puckering white that ran from his eye to his jaw. She saw a dark handsome man with silver-flecked hair, burning eyes and noble features offering her protection from utter loss and desolation and grief.

He stood tall and still, his arms at the sides of his lean body. 'Joanna!' His voice was warm and husky. He opened his arms to her and without thinking, she went willingly to him as if she belonged there and pressed her face against the firm warmth of his chest. He crushed her to him and she knew she was safe. His body was warm against her and she heard him murmur something in Spanish against her hair. She couldn't begin to understand what he was saying, but it didn't matter. Nothing else mattered but that she was here, she was with him, and she was safe.

CHAPTER THREE

JOANNA never knew how long she stayed wrapped in Don Rafael's arms. She didn't hear Manuel tactfully withdraw. She only knew that never before had she felt so safe and secure. When she finally leaned away from him, he kept her within the circle of his arms and wiped the tears from her cheeks with his fingers.

'I'm all right now,' she murmured in a low voice that shook. Gathering herself together, she lifted her chin and looked him straight in the eye with all the courage she could muster. 'What must I do?'

Deep admiration gleamed in his smile. 'First we must contact the police and tell them you are safe, that you were not in the plane after all.'

'How will I explain—about Roger?'

'Do not worry, *niña*. The truth can be whitewashed a little. Trust me.' His tone was wry when he reluctantly turned away and retreated behind his desk.

In practically no time at all he reached the police on the telephone. She heard him speaking rapidly in Spanish, but she could only understand snatches of the one-sided conversation. The deep rich timbre of his voice was strangely comforting. She knew instinctively there was nothing to worry about now that he was in charge.

Manuel came back to the study with Josefa just as Don Rafael hung up the receiver.

'The chief of police wishes to express his relief that you are unhurt, Joanna. However, there are a few formalities that must be taken care of first thing tomorrow.' He nodded to Manuel and Josefa. 'Joanna and I will leave immediately after breakfast.'

'You, Don Rafael?' Josefa whispered, her eyes wide in surprise.

'Since our guest is under my protection, I, too, must fill out the inevitable government forms.' He spoke quietly but firmly as though it was not at all an unusual occurrence for him to leave his home and go in to Malaga. He turned to his brother. 'Manuel, you must stay here and see that no newspaper reporters disturb our privacy. This is bound to cause a great deal of speculation. You will tell them nothing, do you understand?'

'*Si*, Rafael,' he nodded slowly.

'Good. Then if you will be so kind as to show Joanna to her room, I am sure she could do with a rest to overcome any ill effects of the shock she has just suffered.

'Josefa,' he went on snapping orders, 'prepare a tray for our guest and take it to her room. I am sure she will not wish to sit through a meal such as she did last night.' When he looked again at Joanna, he quirked an eyebrow but his voice had the ring of command. 'I hope you sleep tonight, *niña*. Please try not to let anything trouble you.'

'I trust you, Don Rafael,' she said quite innocently in a clear voice before they all left the room.

If he thought her comment unusual, he gave no indication of it.

Manuel was all grave concern when he gently ushered Joanna upstairs. He stopped outside her door and murmured quietly: 'I hope you will rest. If you need anything at all, do not hesitate to ask.' He squeezed both her hands in his.

She looked up into his dark face and forced a small smile. 'Thank you. I don't know what I would have done without you.'

She heard him go as she stood at the half-open door to her room, then everything was quiet and still. Pushing open the heavy door, she crossed the room and stood by the window looking out into the deepening dusk. Mechanically her eyes roamed over the barely visible hills and settled on the dim twinkle of lights from the village in the distance. She leaned her forehead against the cool glass and closed her eyes as silent tears began to spill from beneath her lashes, the full force of the tragedy hitting her like a painful blow.

Roger Thornton was dead. His brother Jack and his best friends were dead. All of them, gone. They had come to Spain seeking sun and laughter, but instead, they had found death on an Iberian mountain in the darkness. *And she should have been with them.*

'Why not me?' The whispered words choked her. 'If I hadn't run away from Roger, I never would have met Manuel and his brother. I would have been with them.' Suddenly she jerked her head back and her eyes widened as the shock struck at her. 'If I hadn't run away, they wouldn't have left. There would have been no need to go. They had plans to stay two weeks!' A fine trembling seized her as the horror of her guilt washed over her. 'It was my fault they died. If I hadn't been such a prude!' She dragged both hands through her hair and stared blindly at the darkness outside the window. She was no longer numb. She felt sick and afraid. 'What have I done!'

Don Rafael's firm purposeful strides were checked in the hall outside her open door. His carved face twisted with compassion when he looked in on her and heard her choked cry. 'You must not think about it, Joanna. Do you hear me?'

But she didn't want to listen. 'I shouldn't have been such an innocent.' She caught her breath on a gulp. 'It's all my fault. Don't you see? It's my fault they died!'

'Stop it!' He came to the window close behind her and dug his fingers punishingly into her shoulders. 'You will make yourself ill. You cannot blame yourself. You had no part in this accident. They were drinking most of the day, were they not?'

Her head dipped mutely.

'Just as drinking and driving do not mix, drinking and flying can be even more deadly. Your friends behaved stupidly and have paid the price for it. You will not blame yourself. It was not your fault they left you and crashed in the mountains.'

There was a curious fluttering in her stomach when he pulled her back against him, holding her so close she could feel his vibrant warmth scorching her. His hands were gentle but firm and he murmured softly, over and over into her hair: 'You must not blame yourself, *pequeña.* It is over, it is done. You are here—you are safe with me.'

Gradually she was again comforted and with a sense of wonder she realised she had no desire to move at all. She drew from his strength, she knew, but it was more than that. She needed him, more than any man she had ever known. She was no longer afraid of him or in awe of his titled nobility. She had to admit to a certain curiosity about him. He was a strange silent man, lonely perhaps, and suddenly she wanted to know all about him, why he stayed alone in this house and what terrible brooding thoughts he had.

She relaxed against him and drew a deep sighing breath. His strong tanned hand slowly brushed against the side of her neck and her every breath made her aware of the warm strength of his fingers stroking the soft whiteness of her skin. She had the most ridiculous desire to turn to him, to hold on to him and tell him she wanted to stay here for ever and never leave him.

'Will you be all right now?' he murmured, his breath warm against her hair.

'When I'm with you, I feel safe. I have nothing to worry

about. But when you're gone . . .' To her ignominy, she turned and flung herself into his arms and pleaded pathetically: 'Don't leave me, Don Rafael. It's so terrible to be alone!'

He folded her close in a searing embrace. 'Hush, *pequeña*. You will never leave me. How could I let you go?'

Josefa came then with a tray and hid her surprise at finding Joanna locked in his arms. They heard her contented sigh when she closed the door behind her, and Don Rafael smiled indulgently before releasing Joanna with obvious reluctance.

'This is a Spanish household and we must obey the rules of propriety,' he said in an oddly thick voice, walking over to the door and opening it again. 'It would not do for me to be alone with you in my wife's bedroom with the door closed.' He glanced around the room as if seeing it for the first time and a flash of pain flickered across his face.

Joanna pushed her hair away from her eyes and struggled to find her composure. 'Your wife's room?'

'*Si*. All the *duquesas* of our family have slept here.'

'You must think I'm terrible!'

He stepped across the thick carpet and sat on the edge of a chair facing her. 'No, little one. Manuel and Josefa put you here purposely. They can be daunting at times, but I do not let it worry me. I have seen through this charade from the start. Manuel intends for you to marry me, did you know that?'

Her jaw dropped and she stared at him. 'I know he was pushing me at you, but I had no idea it was to go that far!'

His eyes narrowed to icy blue-black slits. 'A successful *matador* must think ahead and plan all his moves in advance, but at the same time he must be prepared for the unexpected and allow for it. Manuel is young yet, but he will learn.' He stood up restlessly and paced the room with a light graceful tread. 'I have not been in this room since the night my wife died. Manuel was fourteen years old then and I was too overcome with my own—grief—to be concerned with his. I have not been a good brother in many ways, but I love Manuel and I know what is best for him.'

His pacing brought him again to the middle of the room where Joanna was standing. He ran his hand along the edge of his scar. 'He means well, I am certain, but he is so transparent. He even tries to have you wear your hair the way Matilda did, as if such a thing matters to me. However, I do not intend to fall in with his wishes. I cannot marry you, Joanna.'

Guilty colour surged to her face and neck. When she had thrown herself into his arms and begged him not to leave her, he must have thought it was all part of Manuel's plan, that she was acting her part to perfection. He was not to know it was an instinctive action. She breathed deeply several times to steady her nerves and stared at the floor. 'I'm sorry, I've really made a fool of myself.'

'No, Joanna. I recognise gratitude when I see it and I do not confuse it with something else. You were only trying to help my brother. But I wish to make our positions clear from the beginning. I shall never marry again, but I do wish to have many nephews to fill this empty house and you can help me. I intend for you to marry Manuel.'

Her head jerked up and she gaped at him. He resented his brother trying to manipulate him, but it was perfectly all right for him to be allowed to do the same to Manuel! 'But I don't love him!'

'Love,' he scoffed. 'It is a foolish emotion that means nothing. You did not love this Roger Thornton, yet you wish you had given in to his demands yesterday. If you had, he might be alive today. Is that not what you think?' His deliberately jeering tone told her he didn't expect an answer. 'What about love, then? It does not enter into any sane conversation. A man must be ruled by his head not his heart.'

'I could never marry a man I didn't love.'

'Oh yes, you will, little one.' A coldly mocking smile twisted his mouth. 'And I will show you that you can find a deep fulfilment in being married to Manuel. In many ways an arranged marriage is much more successful than one in which the husband and wife "love" each other. You said before that you trust me. That is all I ask—trust me. I will teach you all you need to know about being the wife of a Spaniard who will one day be a *duque*.' He turned towards the door. 'Try to rest now, Joanna. I have said too much too soon, I know, but I wanted to give you something else to think about rather than dwelling on unpleasant things. Rest now and let nothing trouble you.' Then he was gone.

She stared at the empty doorway and felt the salty flood of tears at the back of her eyes as reaction set in. How could she let nothing trouble her? She didn't want to marry Manuel. He was only eighteen! Only five years separated them, but she felt more like his mother in some ways. She could never be his wife! A desperate little laugh escaped her. It was absurd. She was here at their mercy, it was true, but no one could force marriage on her. Such a thought was ridiculous.

What an impossible household! Manuel wanted a wife for Rafael; Rafael wanted a wife for Manuel. She was a total stranger, and yet each one intended to marry her to the other!

She sat on the edge of the bed and buried her face in her hands. 'When I marry, it will be to the man of my own choosing,' she whispered. 'And I will never choose to marry Manuel.'

She slept fitfully and as dawn began to purple the sky on the distant horizon, she stood by the window looking down the sweeping green length of the hillside, listening to the gentle murmur of the sea. Her usually bright blue eyes were shadowed with pale purple circles as they rested on the huddle of the village houses at the base of the hill and in the distance she heard the dim murmur of church bells calling the simple people to early Mass. She closed her eyes and moved away from the tranquil scene outside.

There would be no more tranquillity for her, she thought wearily. She was tired and out of sorts because she barely slept even though she was exhausted. In spite of the startling announcement that Don Rafael intended to make her his sister-in-law, thoughts of Roger kept crowding in. She had been his secretary for two years and all during that time she thought he was a good kind man. It had taken this trip to Spain to show her how self-centred he really was. Now he was dead and she didn't feel devastated because she would never see him again. A sudden guilt rushed through her. Why should she still be alive when he was dead? Roger meant nothing to her, but she really ought to feel something besides this guilt and this hollow emptiness. Had she always been so shallow?

With her eyes closed, Rafael Santiago's dark brooding face wavered before her. Ever since the first moment she met him, she had thought of no one else. Roger became a dim shadow beside the powerful figure of Don Rafael. Even Manuel couldn't compete with his brother. Always his young boyish face was replaced by an older, more striking countenance with the ragged white scar snaking down his cheek. A shudder passed over her slim body.

'He can't force me to do anything I don't want to do,' she muttered. 'He knows I don't love Manuel. He can't force me to marry him.'

Even as she showered and dressed in the crisp white sundress he paid for yesterday, she said the words over and over like a litany. 'He can't force me.'

Her bed was quickly straightened before she descended the staircase, and she grimaced when she remembered how late she slept yesterday morning. Roger had been dead by then, she shuddered, but she had been blithely unaware.

When she reached the bottom of the stairs, she met Manuel coming in the front door. '*Buenos dias*, Manuel.'

'*Buenos dias*. You are up early.'

'I couldn't sleep. What's your excuse?'

'I am just returning from early Mass,' he smiled sheepishly. 'I go every day.'

'Such devotion is rare where I come from—but then Spain is a very religious country, is it not?'

'Not everyone is Catholic here, but in villages this size, we are in the majority.' He grinned and put a casual arm across her shoulders and started towards the kitchen. 'Even Rafael is a good Catholic when it suits him. But even so, Father Esteban prays daily for the salvation of his soul. I told him about you this morning, and he wishes me to tell you that he will keep you also in his prayers so that you will have the courage to face what is ahead of you.'

Joanna gulped. Did he realise what was ahead of her? 'Please thank him for me, will you?'

'You will have an opportunity to meet him and thank him yourself,' he said, pushing open the kitchen door. 'He is coming here this evening. He wishes to meet the beautiful English *señorita* from America.'

For a numbed moment she could only stare at him.

'Who—who invited him?' Surely Don Rafael wasn't setting up this meeting with the village priest who would probably perform the marriage ceremony? He wouldn't be so premature! She wouldn't marry Manuel no matter what!

'Joanna, your face is so white. What is it?'

She sank down on to a chair. 'I'm sorry.' Her trembling fingers brushed against her eyes. 'Who did you say invited the priest?'

He frowned for a moment, then went to the refrigerator and poured two glasses of orange juice. 'I did. He expressed a desire to meet the woman who has changed my brother into a human being again.'

'Please, Manuel—I haven't done any such thing. I'm a stranger who happened to be stranded in your country. Your brother offered me a glimpse of Spanish hospitality, nothing more. He would do the same for anyone in the same situation.'

He smiled awkwardly and apologised before lapsing into a steady stream of Spanish she couldn't even begin to understand.

Josefa bustled into the room and blinked in surprise. '*Buenos dias, señorita*—Manuel. I will have breakfast ready soon.'

Utter despair washed over her. 'Don't hurry, Josefa. I haven't any appetite.'

But she managed to eat some of the light breakfast set before her and when she finally pushed the plate away, Josefa sighed. 'I simply can't eat any more,' Joanna said softly, and stood up.

'If you have finished, Don Rafael will meet you in the courtyard,' the little woman said softly, putting her gnarled hand timidly on Joanna's arm to detain her. 'When you go into the city, you will—you will——' she stammered.

'Many curious looks will come your way, Joanna,' Manuel cut in smoothly. 'What Josefa is trying to say is please try to be kind to Rafael. He is risking a great deal by taking you himself. He could just as easily have had the police come here.'

Joanna swallowed. 'Then why——?'

He shrugged his shoulders. 'It is time he was out in the public eye again. Perhaps he feels more confident in the company of so beautiful a woman. The stares will be directed at you and not at him.'

'No,' she protested in angry despair, 'there must be some other reason.' Closing her eyes tightly, she turned her back to them. 'I don't want to do anything that might cause him to be hurt—and I'll tell him so.'

But Don Rafael wouldn't hear of any objection to going into Malaga. Swiftly and decisively he cut her off in mid-sentence. Standing quite rigid in a severe black suit with a white shirt and grey tie in the brilliant sun-dappled courtyard, he merely gripped her elbow and propelled her towards the car.

'Please get in, *señorita*, we have a long ride ahead of us.' His voice was taut and he swung the door open with controlled violence.

She was forced to obey and the car shot forward like a blinding black streak down the narrow road.

The silence between them was tangible and to her annoyance, she felt her gaze straying from his long dark fingers with their firm grip on the steering wheel to his grim brooding profile. A wave of heat swept through her and she shivered at his nearness. His hair gleamed darkly with the fine silver threads at the temples and became slightly ruffled in the breeze from his open window. The woody tang of his shaving lotion and the aroma of tobacco clung to him, and suddenly the scent of him and the scent of the earth and the sea all seemed to be mixed up together. He was the essence of Spain.

Joanna tore her eyes away from him and stared at her hands twisted tightly together in her lap. It must be gratitude I feel, she told herself. It can't be anything else. The feeling of futility struck at her and made her sick.

The powerful car slowed almost to a crawl as they wound their way through the narrow streets of the village. Children were playing with cheerful abandon in open doorways and the streets were teeming with bustling activity. It was an effort to turn her attention away from her own troubles, but she looked at the people lingering by the side of the road and saw many shy waves of greeting when the villagers recognised the car and the dark proud Duke behind the wheel. He did not return the salute but merely inclined his head with a haughty dignity and carefully guided the car through the dusty streets.

They passed the house on the outskirts where yesterday a woman had ducked in the doorway, and Joanna saw a brief flash of pain cross his arrogant set features. Was he remembering the last time he came here when someone had screamed when she saw him? Deep compassion welled up in her, but she didn't dare utter a sound. He wouldn't tolerate her compassion, she knew. He probably wouldn't understand such an emotion applied to himself, so she merely sat beside him in the tense silence and waited for him to speak first.

After a lapse of a good fifteen minutes, the grimness left his expression. 'You are a very unusual woman,' he said quietly. 'You do not talk a man to death.'

She coloured delicately. 'I really haven't anything to say.'

'When did that ever stop a woman?' He flicked back his cuff and looked at the plain gold watch on his wrist. 'You have been silent a long time. I wonder what thoughts have run through that beautiful head of yours.'

She devoured the indulgent smile on his lips, then shrugged her shoulders artlessly. 'I was just drinking in the beauty of the countryside, storing up impressions to take home with me.'

'But you are not a tourist. You will have this view whenever you wish for the rest of your life.'

'I am going home,' she said firmly.

'You told me there was nothing, no one waiting for you in America.' His face hardened into harsh forbidding lines. 'Did you lie to me?'

'No, I didn't lie. There's no one—but I can't do what—what you've planned for me. I don't love Manuel, and if that isn't enough, you must know I'm not suited to a life of nobility. I'm just a poor working girl. Your life and mine are poles apart.' She looked into his dark face and saw his implacable set jaw and couldn't suppress a shiver. 'How can I make you understand?'

Don Rafael turned back to the road to concentrate on avoiding the deep ruts, but not before she was given the full benefit of the glittering anger in his eyes. 'I didn't realise you are a snob.'

'Snob?'

'Is that not the correct word? Do you not feel your position to be inferior to mine and so you must twist it until you no longer find yourself beneath me? Is that not why you are refusing to even consider what I am offering you?'

'You merely offered hospitality to me when I found myself in need of your assistance. I came into your life uninvited. You don't know anything about me except that I'm here on holiday. There's absolutely no reason for you to expect me to become a part of your family. It doesn't make any sense. You can't order me to marry your brother.'

'Cannot I order?' The clipped words came from between his teeth in a savage jumble and he broke off with difficulty, suddenly reverting to his native tongue.

Joanna winced and her breath caught at the back of her throat as the storm of anger swept over her.

Abruptly Don Rafael pulled off to the side of the road and switched off the engine, bending his head while trying to control the swift surge of temper. 'I apologise, *señorita.*' He breathed deeply and straightened to look at her. 'I am not good with the English when I am upset. I have been insensitive. You are faced with a very unpleasant meeting with the authorities this morning and I thought to take your mind off it by giving you something else to think about. I did not realise the idea of being married to Manuel is so abhorrent to you.'

'Then you didn't really mean it?' She looked at him in relieved surprise. 'You were only joking?'

'No, it is no joke. I am quite serious. But I should have waited longer before making my plans known.'

'Oh, won't you understand?' she said fiercely. 'I don't intend to marry anybody and you can't force me. I should get you and Manuel together and tell you both once and for all—I resent being manipulated. He's pushing me at you, you're pushing me at him. I don't want any part of either of you!' To her utter humiliation, bright tears rolled down her cheeks and she couldn't hold back a sob of anguish. Turning her head away, she tried to hide the damning tears. Then she started violently when his fingers closed over her arms, dragging her across the seat closer to him. His warm breath fanned her face and she tried to twist away.

'Joanna, listen to me.' His fingers tightened. 'I am trying to tell you—I understand——'

'You don't! You'll never understand.'

'Stop it! You must listen to me.'

Her sobs became harsh and racking, her bright head

bending forward like a fragile gold blossom on a broken stem. It was too much for him to see her this way and he gathered her roughly into his powerful arms and rained gentle kisses on her forehead, her eyes and cheeks before coming to rest on the startled softness of her mouth.

Strange sensations feathered along her nerves. Instead of pulling away, a desire to cling to him, to lose herself in his warmth and strength burned steadily as her lips quivered in instinctive response. Involuntarily she moved against him, her hands straying up towards his neck.

At once he broke away from her. 'Forgive me,' he said in a controlled voice.

'No, I won't forgive you.' Her rounded eyes brightened with shimmering tears. 'Why should I forgive you for the first uncalculated move you've made since I met you?'

He blinked in surprise, but a glimmer of unwilling admiration lurked in his eyes and his fingers bumped carelessly along his scar. 'I never know where I am with you. You are much like an obstinate young bull in the arena when the *matador* sees him for the first time being lured by the capes. At the moment, I cannot tell what you will do, so I am unable to control you. But I like a fighting animal, one that is not afraid of charging hard and straight. I shall be on the alert and in the end I will give you the kiss of steel, one broad swift stroke of the sword, and then . . .'

Joanna shuddered uncontrollably. 'Oh, don't! I'm not one of your bulls, *señor matador*. You'll never bring me to my knees.'

'Is that a challenge?' His soft voice became menacing even as he wryly acknowledged her audacity. He stared at her and straightened, settling himself smoothly behind the wheel.

She could feel the tension between them flare. 'If you want to consider it a challenge, then it shall be. I will not marry Manuel!'

His stare hardened, but apart from a tightening of his lips when he swung back on to the road, he made no further comment.

She would never let him force that marriage on her no matter how hard he tried. With a faint sigh she closed her eyes and leaned back wearily against the leather seat. All this fencing with him made her weak. She was out of her depth and she knew it, but she would never give in.

In a seemingly short time the car was parked on a tree-lined street and Don Rafael directed her along a narrow alley. 'There may be reporters eager to question you, but you will tell them nothing,' he commanded. 'I will try to make this as easy for you as possible.' His voice was curt and his fingers gripped hers as he went ahead, threading his way between small groups of bustling shoppers, tourists and sightseers.

Through the broad sweep of her lashes Joanna saw the grim line of tension that tightened his lips, but no one took note of their progress down the crowded alleyway and she was thankful for small favours. The warm firm strength of his grip was reassuring, but she couldn't control the involuntary tremor that ran through her at the thought of what was in store for her.

'Do not be afraid, *niña*,' he said huskily. 'Trust me.'

They turned into a nearby glass doorway and entered a dingy room that smelled of stale tobacco smoke and a strong disinfectant.

'Through this hallway,' he directed her. 'Sergeant Rivera is a friend of mine. We should be able to have a few moments of privacy before the press find out we have come in the back door.'

It was after three o'clock when they emerged from the office to the barrage of reporters and flashbulbs that momentarily blinded them. Joanna shrank back against

Don Rafael and immediately his arm tightened around her shoulders, banishing her impulse to flee from the questions that were flung at her in halting English she couldn't understand.

With a complete disregard for his own obsession for privacy, Don Rafael spoke firmly in his rich quiet voice, explaining her presence at his home rather than on the plane with her American friends. She felt herself return the sudden deprecating smiles that the newspaper men showered on her without really knowing why. They bowed politely to her and shook Don Rafael's hand with a deference reserved for his nobility, and within a matter of minutes the noisy crowd dispersed.

Don Rafael turned to the police chief and shook his hand firmly with a slight aloof smile. '*Muchas gracias*, Rivera.'

'Any time, *amigo*. Take care of the little *novia*.' He nodded and grinned, and moved his corpulent frame back into his office.

Joanna looked at Don Rafael questioningly, but he merely gripped her elbow and led her out into the brilliant sunshine.

'It was not so terrible, was it? I told you, you must trust me.'

The heat was merciless when they emerged from the police station and threaded their way down the busy packed street. Several curious stares were directed their way, but he remained blind and deaf to everything around them. When once again they reached the relative privacy of his car, he allowed himself to relax and, opening the door, he bowed politely. 'Come, *señorita*, we will have our afternoon meal without the cynosure of horrified eyes. Josefa has provided us with a picnic.'

Joanna found it difficult to get used to the late meal-times of this country, but she found that since her ordeal with the Spanish police department was over, her appetite was beginning to return and was making itself known by the loud rumblings of her stomach.

They drove past the grim walls of the eleventh-century fortress of Gibralfaro and continued out of the city, turning on to a heavily rutted road that branched away from the blaring noise of tourist traffic on the highway. The idyllic spot Don Rafael chose for their picnic had to be the most beautiful place in Spain, and she told him so.

'I am glad you like it, *pequeña.*' He took the edge of the blanket from her and helped to spread it on the thick grass beneath a low shady tree, then opened the hamper and together they set out plates and napkins.

Josefa had provided substantial chicken salad sandwiches and fresh fruit and several different kinds of cheese for them, but a frown creased Don Rafael's forehead when he pulled the last item from the hamper, a bottle of dry white wine.

'We have no glasses.'

'It doesn't matter, really. I'd rather not drink any wine.' Joanna bent to straighten the blanket and hoped he would think the redness in her cheeks was caused by exertion rather than a blush.

He set the bottle down, removed his jacket and tie and unbuttoned his shirt part way before stretching his length with unhurried grace on the lush grass that sloped down to the sea. 'You must not worry that you will get sick every time you drink wine, Joanna.'

Her head jerked up and she stared at him.

'I am sure it was a combination of jumpy nerves and an empty stomach that caused you to become so violently ill.'

'*You knew?*'

His lips twitched in a slight smile. 'The bathroom has a connecting door to my rooms. I would have to have been deaf to be unaware of your predicament.'

She put her hands to her burning cheeks. 'I must have given you a very bad impression of myself—you must have thought I was no better than Roger and his friends. You probably think we're all alike.'

'So far I have found you refreshingly different. You handled yourself quite well under the circumstances.'

He stretched his legs lazily and settled himself on his back on the grass with his eyes closed. A slight breeze ruffled his hair and began to ripple across the fine white material of his shirt. He had rolled back his sleeves almost to his elbows, and while Joanna silently finished her meal, her eyes lingered on the powerful muscles of his arms. He was deceptively lean, she realised, and she couldn't help staring at the way his shirt outlined the bulging muscles of his chest. His breathing became deep and evened into a steady rhythm. His face with its proud carved lines was no longer etched with controlled hauteur. Now he looked incredibly young, and once again she thought he was the most compellingly handsome man she had ever met. The livid white streak slashing across his cheek only added to his handsomeness. In no way did it detract from his startling dark looks.

In order to resist the sudden mad impulse to reach out and stroke his face, she forced herself to gather up the remains of the picnic and put them back in the hamper, all the while trying to be quiet so as not to wake him.

Perhaps today had been more of a strain on him than she imagined. He was no longer used to being in the public eye, but he had braved the curious stares of strangers and the blinding glare of flashbulbs in order to protect her. Her heart swelled and she felt that she would never be more in love with him than she was at this moment. Could it be love? she wondered. It had happened so fast. I only met him two days ago, she thought, yet I feel as if I've known him all my life.

She drew her knees up under her chin and let her eyes wander over his face. When he was completely relaxed like this, he looked so young. If only he could love me! she thought with futility. It would be heaven just to be here with him on this glorious Spanish hillside. But he doesn't. He wants me to marry Manuel. Never!

The breeze whispered all around them and the sun continued on its silent arc across the sky. Joanna became so engrossed in her contemplation of him that she didn't realise how much time had passed. She was still looking at him with deep fascination when his long dark lashes blinked open to look directly into her face and her heart began to thump madly against her ribs.

'Forgive me, *señorita*. It was most impolite to fall asleep like this.' He gave her an embarrassed grin. 'Perhaps it is because I find your company soothing. You are not like any woman I have ever known.' He shook his head as if wondering why he even said such a thing and turned on his side towards her.

'I'm like an old shoe,' she sighed. 'My father always thought so, anyway.'

'I am sure he meant that as a compliment. Not many men find the company of a woman relaxing. You loved him very much, did you not?'

'Yes. He was my father, but he was also my best friend. I could talk to him about anything and he'd understand. Do you know what I mean?'

He studied the wistful sadness in her face for a moment and smiled a little. 'Yes. You have been very fortunate. Few people find such a kindred spirit in their lifetime.'

Their eyes met and held as they looked at each other with an eloquence that needed no words, and time and space suddenly dissolved. And then she knew that he, too, was lonely. A flicker of pain passed over his face and the contact was abruptly broken.

'You miss your father very much, do you not?'

She nodded, not trusting herself to speak.

'Will you allow me to take his place?'

'You?'

'*Si*. I never had a daughter, but if I had, I would very much hope she would be like you.'

'A daughter?' She pressed her hands to her face. 'My father was sixty-two when he died, Don Rafael, and he had snow-white hair. You're nowhere near that age and I could never begin to consider you as a father.' I love you too much as a man, she wanted to add, but didn't.

'There are so many things I could teach you.'

A bitter sigh escaped her. 'Is that how you see me? I'm a child who needs to be taught?'

'You are very young and not used to our ways. If you will not think of me as a father, then I shall be your——' he searched for the word and snapped his fingers when he found it, '——mentor. I am older and wiser and I know what is best for you and Manuel. I could take care of you. Will you allow it?'

'My mentor,' she said, shivering, 'who will teach me many things.' There was infinite sadness in her face when she turned away. Can you teach me not to love you? her heart cried.

With an effortless movement, Don Rafael sat up, reaching out to capture her chin, turning her face to his to study her strained features. 'Well, Joanna?'

'You're only a few years older than I am. Why do you pretend you're so ancient?'

'I am much older than my twenty-eight years. I have seen things and done things other people only dream about. Actually I am an old man—old enough to be your mentor.'

'Do I have any other choice?'

He smiled brilliantly. 'Ah, Joanna. Our relationship will grow on you. You will have no regrets. Trust me, I will teach you so many things.'

'Will you teach me Spanish?' She spoke huskily and leaned away from him.

'But of course. Is there any particular phrase you wish to know?'

Joanna shrugged her shoulders artlessly, pretending to consider, then looked into his eyes seizing on the one word that stayed in her consciousness from this afternoon's encounter with the police. 'Sergeant Rivera said, "Take care of the little *novia.*" I've heard you call me *niña* and *pequeña* and I assume they mean "little one" or "little girl" or something like that. But what is *novia*?'

Immediately the flash of indulgent amusement faded from his eyes. He stood and deliberately rolled his sleeves down slowly, fastening them at his wrists with small gold cufflinks. He shrugged into his coat and again knotted his tie. 'It is time for us to return home. Manuel will be waiting,' he said coldly.

'What did I say?' Joanna scrambled to her feet, blinking in confusion, startled and chilled by his sudden change of attitude. 'What does the word mean?' Her heart began to beat in thick strokes as a nasty suspicion entered her mind. As she faced him squarely, the challenge in her darkening eyes hardened. 'Would you rather have me ask Manuel when we get back?'

He took a cheroot from his pocket and cupped his hand over the flame, shielding it from the breeze as he lit it, taking an inordinate amount of time to complete the task. He looked into her questioning face with controlled indifference. '*Novia* means betrothed,' he said quietly.

Her heart stopped as if it had become a frozen fist in the middle of her chest. 'No!' The word broke from her ashen lips and an uncontrollable shiver raced down her spine. 'No! You *couldn't*! You *wouldn't*!' She tore her stunned gaze away from the cold glitter of his eyes. Her breathing became constricted and she raised dazed hands to her face. 'And the reporters? You told them too? That's why they smiled and bowed and shook my hand?'

'Believe me, Joanna, it is for the best. Manuel is a dutiful boy. You both will take your rightful place in the Santiago family. Just think, one day you will become Duquesa Joanna.'

'Oh, don't talk like that!' She couldn't bear to think of herself married to Manuel. 'I won't marry him! I don't want to become a *duquesa*.' A sob was torn from her throat and she turned on him with outraged fury. 'And to think I trusted you, my mentor!'

'That is enough,' he said stonily, his arrogant head tilted upward, his lean muscular body taut as if waiting for a bull to charge. 'I have done nothing to betray that trust. Why do you think everything went so smoothly today? If it had not been for the fact that you are betrothed to my brother, you would have found it extremely difficult to explain your presence here without your friends. There might have been the suspicion that it was not really an accident, no? I simply made it easier for you. I explained that your parents were old friends of my family and there had been an understanding between us for many years.'

'But that's a lie!'

'Let us just say I stretched the truth. You and I had the understanding. I told you last night, I intended for you to marry Manuel. As your brother-in-law, I will teach you to become a *duquesa* with all the flair necessary to the position.'

'No! That isn't something that can be taught. I could never become a duchess,' she cried bitterly, deliberately using the English version of the word to irritate him.

But it had no effect on him. He stood tall and still, regarding her coldly against the backdrop of the brilliant green hillside.

Her eyes widened as she stared steadily back at him. 'Oh, I can see it all so clearly now. Yesterday, before we went to shop for the clothes you wanted me to have, I told you you didn't have to spend money on me, but you said you'd do anything to keep—*your brother in line*. He's giving you trouble, isn't he? He's not ready to settle down yet, but you're forcing him so you can have nephews to inherit your wealth. Isn't that right? I didn't realise you'd stoop so low as to try to buy him a wife.'

'Every woman has her price, *señorita*.'

'You can't buy me!'

Her statement brought no reaction. He merely bent down and gathered up the blanket and hamper and started towards the car with an unhurried feline grace that infuriated her.

CHAPTER FOUR

By the time they returned to Don Rafael's villa, lines of strain were etched on Joanna's stricken face. A tight-lipped silence settled between them during the long drive back, leaving her preoccupied with finding a way to become unengaged to Manuel. The only solution that came to mind was to leave Spain. But how? How could she get away? Where could she go? Who would help her?

Her thoughts whirled, stretching her nerves raw, and a dull throbbing ache settled at her temples. This can't be happening. It's too absurd, she told herself.

There were no newspaper reporters waiting when the

car finally glided to a stop outside the courtyard. She slid from the seat into the warm dusk before Don Rafael could come around and open her door. She avoided looking at him and held her breath when he came to stand beside her, waiting for Manuel to unlock the heavy wrought iron gate.

For the first time since they left the hillside, Don Rafael spoke quietly to her in a cool emotionless voice: 'During our absence I had Josefa prepare a different room for you. It was highly improper to use my wife's room, you understand?' His lips twisted, but he did not wait for an answer. 'Our aunt, Isabel Montoya, will arrive some time this evening to act as your *duena*, so all the proprieties will be observed.'

'*Duena?*' she gasped.

The contemptuous look he threw her was meant to silence her, but seeing him stand so still and straight with his feet planted firmly in front of him, she reacted with all the violence of a young bull when a red cape is waved in the ring.

'There is no need, Excellency! I won't be here that long!'

'Miss Taylor, may I remind you that you are under my care and I am responsible for you?'

'And I'm supposed to sit still and allow you to force me into a marriage I don't want? This is marriage we're talking about, not some holiday that will last a week or two. Marriage is for life—and it's my life!'

'Enough!'

His thundering scowl did nothing to deter her. 'Oh no, it's not enough, Excellency!' Goaded beyond reason, she raised her hand and felt a sudden tingling sensation all the way down her arm as her hand slashed across his scarred cheek.

He did not move a muscle and instantly she was filled with a dull sense of dread. 'Did that make you feel better, Miss Taylor?' he asked with infuriating calmness. His expression did not change and he did not raise a hand to his face where the red outline of her handprint looked peculiar against the stark white streak of his scar.

'No,' she choked.

Manuel had been standing silently behind the gate during this entire incident, and now he swung the heavy wrought iron open in an effort to break the tension between them.

'Manuel,' Don Rafael said curtly, 'please show Miss Taylor to her room.' With a nod of dismissal he retreated with an unhurried stride to his car and drove away to the garages.

After he had gone, Manuel squeezed her elbow gently and she flinched at the contact. He was a good kind gentle boy, and that was all he could ever be to her. 'I must talk with you, Joanna,' he said with quiet urgency. 'Please, it is very important.'

A wave of despair swept over her and she sighed, letting him guide her into the house. 'We have much to discuss,' she agreed grimly, trying to swallow the tightness that gripped her throat.

The heels of her sandals clattered discordantly on the marble as they went through an arched hallway on the opposite side of the house to a room smaller than the one she had occupied previously. But it, too, was furnished with elegant simplicity. The high ceiling was beamed and the walls were painted in an ivory texturised paint that gave them a stuccoed effect. Pale blue curtains had been drawn across the long windows which Manuel now parted, flooding the room with the muted light of dusk.

'I hope everything went well with the police today,' he began hesitantly, turning from the window.

'Oh yes,' she said bitterly, staring blindly at her hands clasped in front of her. 'I didn't have to say anything. Your brother did all the talking. I merely signed my name to all the forms wherever he indicated.' A caustic little laugh escaped her. 'Like a blind fool, I trusted him.'

'Joanna——' Manuel stopped and rubbed his hand across the back of his neck, finding it difficult to say what was on his mind.

She turned her haggard face up to him. 'You must help me get away from here, Manuel.'

'Get away? But where do you wish to go?'

'Anywhere—it doesn't matter. Oh, don't you see? I've got to leave here. I can't stay. You—you don't know what happened.' Her breath caught on a sob.

'Yes, I do,' he murmured gently.

'Do you know what he told the authorities and the reporters? He told them we were engaged, you and I. He beat you at your own game, Manuel. By telling the newspaper reporters I'm your *novia,* he thinks he has me trapped. Oh, he can't do this!' She buried her face in her hands. 'Please help me to find a way to leave here!'

He stepped closer to her and took both her hands away from her face. 'You do not have any feelings for me, Joanna? There is no way you could marry me?'

Through a haze of tears she saw that his grim face was quite pale. 'I'm fond of you and I'd never want to hurt you, but I could never be your wife. I'm sorry if I'm hurting your feelings.'

'You do not hurt me with the truth. I feel the same.' He gripped her fingers tightly and drew her to a chair near the window, forcing her to sit. 'I have deliberately acted like an intractable child at times because I wanted you to see how unsuitable I would be as a husband.' His thumbs traced a circular pattern on the back of her hands as he knelt on the floor in front of her, staring into her stricken face. 'You see, Joanna, I have never wanted to marry anyone. I have wanted to become a priest for as long as I can remember.'

'A priest!'

His lips twisted with bitterness. '*Si.* But my brother has other plans for me. He used to argue with my father about it all the time. I am the only heir now, the proud bearer of the Santiago name to whom all society's blessings will flow. Not for me the simple life of a village priest. No, I must marry and have children so the proud name of Santiago will not lie in the dust forgotten.'

Joanna bent her head and stared at the floor miserably. 'I had no idea.'

'My brother is a young man, young enough to have many children of his own. I need not be the last of the Santiago line.' He put his fingers beneath her chin and forced her head up to look into his burning eyes. 'I know you care for him—I have seen it in the way you look at him. You can give him many fine sons.'

'You don't know what you're saying,' she shivered.

'May God forgive me for what I have done.' His hands dropped to his sides as he knelt on the floor at her feet. 'I have prayed for a miracle so I might realise my vocation. I must become a priest. God guided me to that ridge to find you and bring you here. He has made it possible for you not to be sickened by my brother's scars. He guided the reporters here today.'

She stiffened. 'What?'

'Oh, Joanna, forgive me for what I have done to you today. Believe me, I did not plan it this way. I thought you would get to know Rafael and after a while fall in love with him.' His eyes filled with pain. 'The newspaper men came this afternoon, wanting to take my picture to print it in tonight's paper along with yours. It is the top story of the day, you see. A *duque* does not have the power he once had, but the people must still have their continuing symbol of aristocracy which remains above its politics. I realised what Rafael must have told them, so I had to do something. I told them they misunderstood. You are *his novia*, not mine!'

A startled silence followed, filling the room. In an instant she was standing, her shadowed eyes staring at him with horrified fixity. 'How could you?'

'I had to do it.' He got to his feet and looked down at he with his pulse beating erratically in his neck. 'You will make a much better wife for my brother than for me. It is all but an accomplished fact now.'

Joanna blinked and shook her head in denial. 'He won't marry me, Manuel. He won't let you get away with it. He knew what you'd planned all along and last night he told me he would never marry again. He feels nothing for me except that I'd make a convenient sister-in-law.'

'It is out of my hands now. The story will be in this evening's paper and I have invited several of his closest friends to dinner tonight. When he sees the news, it will be too late and in front of too many people. He is a man of great pride. It is that which will force him to remain silent.'

'You can't be serious? Nothing will stop him!'

'It must. You know his pride is no small thing.'

Conflicting emotions chased across her face as she stared at him, horrified at his cunning. He wanted to become a priest and he didn't care who was hurt in the process as long as he achieved his own purpose.

'Oh, you've been very clever, haven't you? It doesn't matter what I feel or what I think. When your brother finds out what you've done, how do you think he's going to feel about both of us? He'll be furious with you and he will utterly despise me.'

'No. He will grow to love you.'

'Stop it! There's no way he'll ever love me. If I'm tricked into marriage with him, he can only hate me.'

'You are letting your emotions cloud your reason. He could never hate you.'

'Don't you see how wrong this is?' she insisted fiercely.

Manuel could only look at her standing so stricken in the middle of the lovely room with the shadows and sunlight dancing in the glossy tendrils of her hair and shimmering over her white face. A slight smile crossed his features. 'You are angry now, but when you have had time to think about it, you will see how right it is.' He stepped to a closet on the far side of the room and flung open the doors. 'Will you do me one more favour this evening?' He rummaged through the dresses hanging in colourful profusion on a long rod and pulled out a long green silk gown, laying it across her bed. 'Will you wear this dress for me?'

Joanna pressed her hands to her mouth and stared at the shimmering gown. 'Whose clothes are these?'

He shrugged his shoulders wearily. 'Rafael thinks of everything. When we came home empty-handed yesterday, he ordered these things for you. They were delivered this afternoon.'

'I don't believe his presumption!' she gasped. 'He thinks this is my price?'

He frowned. 'I do not know what you mean.'

'He thought he could buy me for you, Manuel. He told me this afternoon that every woman has a price. He thinks this closetful of clothes is the price he has to pay to make me fall in with his wishes.'

'But you must be mistaken.'

'No, it's your brother who's mistaken. I won't be bought. Fine clothes aren't everything. Living in a palace and being called duchess doesn't mean a thing to me.'

Manuel grinned a sheepish grin, showing his strong white teeth. 'You are beautiful when you are angry. I was the only one who dared to thwart Rafael before. Now you. You will help me?'

'No! How can you even ask?'

'Please. It is most important to me. I will never be happy unless I become a priest.' His dark eyes pleaded with her. 'And you will never know true happiness until you belong to Rafael.'

Joanna turned away from him. 'How can I make you understand? You must know this is going to blow up in your face. Have you thought of that?'

'But how can it? I have thought of everything.' He glanced at the gold watch on his wrist. 'I must leave now. The boy from the village who brings the newspaper should be coming soon, and I must reach him first.' Smiling grimly, he walked to the door. 'The bathroom is at the end of the hall. When you have changed, Josefa will come to you.' And then he was gone.

Joanna looked at the fragile green gown and choked back a sob. Everything was happening too fast. She was trapped in a tangled web of confusion, torn between two men neither of whom wanted her for himself. This can't be happening, she thought again. A man doesn't marry a woman because he's forced to save his pride. This is the twentieth century and there are laws to protect people like me. If only I'd never come here . . .

Half an hour later, after a bath that did nothing to soothe her nerves, she drew a thin cotton wrapper around herself and stood in the darkened room by the window breathing in the cool, flower-scented night air. The sea was on this side of the house, but the gentle murmur of the waves did nothing to calm her.

Manuel had been clever, but she knew Don Rafael was even more so. He would let nothing stand in his way. Even though Manuel had turned the tables on him, he would think of something and she'd be forced to marry Manuel. She just knew it. Something would happen and she would find herself married to a boy who wanted to be a priest. Her brain whirled and her fingers clutched at the pale blue curtains, wrinkling the fragile material. There had to be some way out of this!

Josefa knocked softly at her door and entered with a quick light step. 'Why are you standing in the dark, *señorita*?'

'I was just listening to the sea,' Joanna said in a shattered voice.

'It is very romantic, yes?'

When she didn't reply, Josefa walked into the room and turned on several lamps. 'Don Rafael always loved the sea too. He used to sail all the time, but when he married Doña Matilda, he had to give it up. She did not like the sea.'

'I can't imagine him doing anything he didn't want to do,' she commented spitefully, turning from the window. 'He must have loved her very much to give up sailing just because she didn't like it.'

'He was forced to give it up to keep peace in the family. She had other interests,' Josefa said wryly. 'She came from a very wealthy family in Madrid. This place was too dull for her—no bright lights, no lively parties with sparkling jewels and ladies in brilliant coloured dresses. There was only lazy sunshine and the gentle murmur of the sea. She hated it. They argued all the time.'

'I don't think you should be gossiping like this, Josefa,' said Joanna in a tight little voice, wrapping her arms around herself, trying to shut out the vision of Don Rafael's brooding face arguing with his wife.

Josefa reached out and touched her sleeve. 'I have brought you some tea to help settle your nerves. Very English, yes? Come and drink it while I brush your hair.' Her smile was kind. 'I am not gossiping, *señorita*,' she added when Joanna seated herself before a mirror. 'I am trying to explain why you should not feel badly about marrying Don Rafael.' She hurried on before Joanna could interrupt. 'I told the reporters that Manuel was right—you are betrothed to Don Rafael. They had misunderstood him. You must realise he has been a lonely man all his life. His marriage to Doña Matilda was arranged when they were children. She was much younger than he was, not in years but in temper.' Her face wrinkled expectantly. 'This is the right word?'

'You mean temperament,' Joanna said, reaching for the tea. 'But you really shouldn't be telling me this. It won't change anything. I could never be a suitable duchess for Don Rafael. I don't even like him!'

Josefa ran the brush through the long golden hair and deftly swung the heavy length into a smooth golden coil at the nape of her neck. 'Oh, you must not say this. You are most suitable. You have much pride and you are very stubborn too. Doña Matilda married him only because her family wanted her to become a *duquesa*. Doña Elena wanted to marry him for his wealth. She did not love him. Only you,' she smiled knowingly, 'you have loved him for himself and not his wealth and position.'

The teacup fell from Joanna's trembling fingers and rolled across the thick carpeting, spreading a dark ugly stain in the ice-blue colour. 'Josefa, please!' Her voice wobbled and became faint.

'Do not look so shattered, *señorita*. You have never been indifferent to him, so I know you do care. It is very flattering to so virile a man as Don Rafael to have a woman love him for himself. You have not seen him as he was, you only know him as he is, and still you love him. I know this no matter how much you deny it.'

Joanna jerked to her feet and swung around, breathing harshly. 'But I don't want to love him! It's futile. He can't love me in return. He told me so. He sees me as a child who'd be better off marrying his brother. And it hurts, because that's all I could ever be to him—a child, a child who can be bought with pretty dresses and the promise of a title. You say his wife was much younger in temperament—well, I'm much younger in experience. I don't move in the same circles he does. There's no place for me here. I'm not his equal. I can't be his wife.'

A swift stab of understanding hit her and the old woman's face seemed to wither before Joanna's eyes. She took a deep breath and turned blindly, as if in slow motion, towards the door. 'I have listened only to Manuel for so long,' she whispered. 'I have given no thought to anyone else. He wants to become a priest more than anything else, but it is wrong to find his vocation at someone else's expense. You are right, *señorita*. Even though you love him, it would be wrong for you to marry Don Rafael if he cannot learn to return that love. I am sorry for my part in all this.' She bent her head and opened the door.

Before she stepped into the hallway, Joanna crossed the room and put her trembling hand on her arm. 'I know you meant well and I thank you for your kindness to me.' She bit her lip and searched the woman's kindly face. 'Will you help me? I've got to leave here, don't you see? It's the only way.'

Josefa looked at her sadly. 'I cannot, *señorita*. I have no money to give you and Don Rafael has your passport. There is no way you can go anywhere in this country without it.'

'How do you know he has it?' Joanna tried to hide her eagerness.

'I saw Don Rafael in the study talking with the police messenger who brought it to him just before I came up to you.'

'I see,' she said, and turned away. 'Thank you, you may have been some help after all.'

A plan began forming in her mind, but she said nothing

more and quietly closed the door behind Josefa before hurrying to the bed to slip on the gown Manuel had chosen for her. The green silk was cut in a Grecian toga style, clasped at one shoulder with a thin gold chain, but she had no interest in her appearance. Her mind was on other things. She found a pair of thin gold-strapped sandals and quickly put them on, then silently left the room.

If she hurried, she just might find her passport and be able to get away from here before Don Rafael had even finished dressing for dinner. It was no way to thank him for his hospitality, but in the long run he would be grateful that she had gone from his life.

He probably put her passport in his desk in the study, she reasoned, as she slowly made her way down the stairs. The banister was cold against her clammy hand, but everything was quiet and still with the pre-dinner hush that had fallen over the entire house. Only her heart was thumping so loud that she thought it surely must be heard all over the hall. She crossed the cold marble floor on tiptoe with unaccustomed stealth.

The heavy door to the study swung open soundlessly and she peered around the dim lamplit room searching for any telltale signs of Don Rafael's presence. Slowly, she let out the breath she had been holding and forced herself to breathe evenly. A slim cigar had been stubbed out in the ashtray on his desk and it was still warm. Good, she thought, he must have just gone upstairs to get changed, so that gives me a little time.

She nervously wiped her hands down the sides of her gown and made her way around the desk. Her heart began to bang against her ribs again when she reached out for the handle to one of the desk drawers. Never before had she done this sort of thing. There was something so vulgar about going through another person's desk, and she bit her lip, struggling with herself. It's the only way, she thought. If I ask him for it, he'll only laugh at me. I have to find my passport and get away from here. She tried not to think what he would say if he could see her rummaging through his drawers. This isn't wrong, she thought. I just want my passport—nothing else. She gripped the handle and jerked the drawer open.

Just as she did, the room was suddenly flooded with light and Don Rafael, dark and alien, stood stiffly in the doorway.

'Are you looking for something, Miss Taylor?'

She slammed the drawer shut and gaped at him. The silence was so profound she thought she could hear the ticking of his wrist-watch—but that was absurd. The furious pounding of her heart in her throat must drown out all other noises. She swallowed and continued to stare at him standing so tall and still in a trim-fitting charcoal grey suit that flattered his lean muscular build. She had miscalculated after all. He had already changed for the evening.

'I do not keep anything of value in my desk drawers,' he said sarcastically. 'I am a wealthy man in many ways. If it is my money you want, you have only to ask for it. You do not have to steal it. I will deny you nothing.' His voice was deadly quiet as he advanced into the room.

With a nervous gesture Joanna put her hands behind her and backed away from him as he stalked her with unrelenting slowness. Cold hatred darkened the harsh planes of his face as he matched her jerky backward steps. Abruptly, she bumped against a wall and felt the coldness of it where her palms were pressed behind her.

'You know I wasn't looking for money,' she whispered, nearly choking from the tightness in her throat.

'I do not believe you. It is what women value most, is it not? No matter how much you have, it is never enough.'

'Please——'

His fingers reached out, tightly gripping her shoulders, paralysing her with his touch. 'I have been waiting for you to show your true colours, Miss Taylor. Like all women, you thought to have the wealth without paying the price for it. And you said you could not be bought! Part of the training of a *matador* is the sharpening of his instincts. He must be swift to pick up vibrations, and I was not wrong about you. You are as greedy as all the rest.'

'You're wrong. I don't want anything except my passport, so that I can leave here.'

'You do not fool me for one instant,' he snapped through his teeth. 'What good would a counterfeit passport be to you? Do you think our Customs inspectors are complete idiots? The document is worthless. You will never leave my country with that piece of paper.' His grip tightened. 'So you thought to rob me, did you? I was in the courtyard waiting for the boy who brings the newspaper when I saw you making your way to my study. Such guilt on your white face!' His voice had become almost savage.

Joanna closed her eyes and shuddered as his fingers dug into her shoulders with punishing fierceness. 'I wasn't trying to steal anything,' she got out jerkily. 'I was only looking for my passport. I didn't know it was counterfeit, believe me. Roger took care of it and I had no idea. Please, I want nothing else, not your wealth—it doesn't mean anything to me. I wouldn't know what to do with it if I had it.' She struggled against him and he let her go with loathing.

A cynical expression twisted his hard carved features and his scar became even more grotesque in the brilliant light. 'I do not care for your acting ability. I am niot fool enough to believe you for one instant. Save the pathos for Manuel, he will appreciate it much more than I.'

Joanna wrung her hands in desperation. 'Please just let me go away from here!'

'Oh no, *señorita*. You came to my study tonight for your own selfish purpose, but all that has changed now. By going through my desk, you have put yourself in my hands, and now I shall use you mercilessly. It is the price you have to pay for your weakness. You shall marry Manuel within a week and you shall give me many nephews. For some reason the boy loves you—and he shall have you!'

'No! You know that's not true. He told me he wants to be a priest!'

'Do not defy me. You cannot win. You should have learned that by now,' he jeered.

She stared at him for several agonised seconds. 'You know I'm no thief—not for one minute do you believe it. You're twisting this to suit yourself. No matter what the cost, you intend Manuel to marry. I just happened to be here so you think you can use me for your own selfish ends. But I won't be used,' she said bitterly, dredging up her courage. 'You think you have it all figured out, don't you?' She flung the words at him. 'Well, you'd better think fast, because your brother has just as much twisted determination as you have!'

His black eyebrows rose in a straight arrogant line and he regarded her with haughty coldness.

Her heart began to pound, but she lifted her chin to face him with all the defiance she could muster. 'Manuel has——'

'Rafael! There you are.' Manuel rushed into the room with a newspaper folded under his arm, followed by a short little man in a black suit with a stiff Roman collar shining starkly against his dark skin. Manuel smiled widely, but Joanna noticed the unnatural pallor beneath his tanned skin and the fine film of perspiration that stood out on his brow. She felt Don Rafael stiffen beside her, but he kept his face carefully expressionless.

'Padre,' Manuel turned to the priest, 'I would like to introduce you to Miss Joanna Taylor. Joanna, this is Father Esteban from the village.'

She breathed deeply and took the priest's hand. 'How do you do, Father,' she said with awkward huskiness.

'Manuel has told me so much about you, *señorita*.' He grinned goodnaturedly. 'He was not exaggerating when he said you are very beautiful.'

A painful blush crept up her neck and she saw a grim satisfaction on Don Rafael's face. 'Manuel is very flattering.'

'Excellency,' Father Esteban bowed formally and extended his hand, 'let me be the first to congratulate you on your exceptional taste. You have chosen the perfect *duquesa*——'

'Padre,' Manuel cut in hastily, 'Tia Isabel arrived a short while ago and is waiting to see you again.' He carelessly tossed the newspaper on to his brother's desk and none too subtly tried to shepherd the priest back to the door. 'Shall we go to the *sala*, Padre? Joanna?' His face lost even more colour when he looked at Rafael's sudden grim expression. 'Don Carlos and Ana should be coming soon and Luis Sanchez is bringing a friend with him also to share in this happy occasion——' His voice wobbled and then trailed away uncertainly.

Don Rafael frowned, clearly puzzled. He should have been warned at once by the strange, barely suppressed note of triumph in Manuel's voice when he named the people who were to be present, but he had no inkling of what his brother had done. All at once his dark face became inscrutable. He did not say a word. He merely stepped past Joanna to his desk, reached across the polished surface and opened the newspaper. There was a thin sudden silence in the room while he searched for the article and read the condemning words. Other than a taut whitening of his lips, he made no outward sign acknowledging that Manuel had succeeded in tricking him. Very slowly, he folded the newspaper and replaced it neatly on the desk without a word.

Then he turned and with a fluid movement he held out his arm to Joanna, waiting impassively for her to come to him.

'Dón Rafael,' she whispered tautly, trying to find her composure.

He flinched when she put her hand on his arm and their eyes clashed, but his voice was strong and firm and clear. 'Manuel is right, Tia Isabel is waiting for us.'

The *sala* was a spacious room and Joanna felt out of her depth here. Muted tapestries hung on the walls with their fine gold threads glinting in the light from two enormous crystal chandeliers at either end of the room. Thick Moorish rugs covered the floor while five long shining windows with wide arches marched across the length of the outside wall and opened on to a formal garden.

She longed to escape into the fragrant coolness of the night, but she was not allowed the respite. After a greeting to Manuel's aunt, Father Esteban went with Manuel to the kitchen to have a few words with Josefa, leaving her alone with Don Rafael and Isabel Montoya to await the arrival of the others.

Seated on a low ivory damask couch next to his aunt, Joanna saw that the woman was in her middle fifties and totally Latin in appearance. Her shining black hair was elegantly styled with broad streaks of grey at her temples which, instead of detracting from her appearance, only served to underline her aristocracy. She was a big woman, dressed in black and holding herself with unconscious dignity. Every time she moved, the diamonds at her throat, wrists and fingers sparkled with a glittering fire all their own.

'When you asked me to come here to chaperone, I did not know it was to be for your benefit, Rafael,' she said in scathing tones, making her disapproval obvious. 'I must say I was shocked when Manuel showed me tonight's newspaper.'

He looked coldly at her. 'Must I remind you that you did not approve of my marriage to your godchild either? Joanna and I have an understanding.'

'But she is no more than a child! One can tell just by looking at her that there must be a great disparity of experience between you.'

'My *novia* is quite aware of our differences. Do not let them concern you.'

Isabel Montoya was not going to be silenced. 'Aside from being much too young for a man like you, she is not even Spanish. You cannot pass her off as your *duquesa*. She would be much more suited to Manuel. There is an unworldliness about them. Perhaps by the time he inherits the title, she would be more like one of us.'

'I am aware of her suitability for Manuel,' he snapped harshly, his ill temper barely concealed. 'However, he has made it abundantly clear that he still wishes to enter the priesthood.'

'I should have thought he would be over that by now.'

'It seems not.'

Joanna squirmed. She hated the way they talked about her as if she wasn't in the room with them. Apart from a condescending *'buenas noches'* from the woman, Isabel Montoya had not said one word to her.

Don Rafael had been standing by a window with his feet set wide apart in an autocratic stance when a sudden smile crossed his face and, to Joanna's surprise, he came to her and took her hand, drawing her close to him. Then he turned to introduce her to his friends who were just entering the room followed by Manuel and the priest. With charm oozing from every pore, he completed the task with marvellous composure under the circumstances.

Carlos and Ana Seguras, Manuel's godparents, were a charming couple in their early forties, elegantly dressed in simple but costly evening clothes. Their eager faces were full of curiosity they couldn't conceal.

Following them was Luis Sanchez, quite a young man, of considerable handsomeness and almost oily grace. Dressed in a trim-fitting dark suit that was very elegant and very expensive, there was something familiar about him, but in the flurry of introductions, Joanna couldn't immediately determine what it was.

Clinging coyly to the young man's arm was a voluptuous, tall woman in her late twenties whose beauty could only be described as classic. The wine red satin of her gown outlined every generous curve of her statuesque body. Long dark hair glistened in deep vibrant waves about her lovely face and her snapping black eyes were vivid with expectancy. There was nothing artificial about her creamy complexion, anyone could see that at a glance. She was glowing with health and vitality, making Joanna suddenly feel small and pale and insignificant. Her eyes flicked over Joanna with surprise and then turned questioningly to Don Rafael.

His grip on Joanna's hand tightened so much that she nearly yelped with the pain of it, but when she glanced up at his face, she stared at him with something like shock, forgetting her own discomfort. His face had drained of colour and he stood rigid in front of the woman, unable to take his eyes away from her. His jaw was taut and his eyes were full of pain.

'Rafe, honey, aren't you going to introduce me to

Manuel's little friend here?' Her voice was undeniably American.

Rafe? Honey?

'Señora Elena Vegas, may I present Joanna Taylor,' he said in a strangled voice.

In the quivering silence Joanna's voice was barely audible. 'How do you do, *señora*,' she said hesitantly. 'You're American?'

With unexpected rudeness, Elena Vegas didn't bother to offer Joanna her hand but kept her eyes on Don Rafael, not hiding an elaborate shudder as her dark eyes slid and bumped over his scar. 'How perceptive of you! I'm from California, actually.' Then she tilted her head in condescension. 'And you? With that hair, you can't be Spanish. How did you manage to find your way to this household?'

'Joanna's parents were friends of mine before they moved to America from England.' The lie came easily to Don Rafael's lips. 'We've had an understanding and today Joanna has graciously consented to become my bride.'

'Your bride? Surely you mean Manuel's?'

'My bride,' he said levelly.

'I don't believe it!' Her voice was filled with incredulous shock. Suddenly she didn't look so self-assured. Her seductive smile looked pasted on her face and she had lost a little of her healthy colour.

'We will be married at the end of the week, and I am looking forward to it with much anticipation.' He smiled brilliantly at Joanna, and only she knew what that smile cost him. Her fingers were already numb from his tight grip, but she scarcely felt the pain any more. Her heart hammered uncomfortably, but she gave him her brightest, widest smile in return.

'Why, congratulations!' Luis Sanchez thumped him on the back. 'You are fortunate to have such a lovely girl for your wife. I had no idea . . .' He turned to Elena. 'Did you, honey?'

She pulled herself together with a tremendous effort. 'No, Lou. I'm just as surprised as you are.'

He blushed scarlet at the mutilation of his name.

'Our betrothal has been announced in tonight's paper,' Don Rafael's eyes were bleak. 'You may not have seen it yet.'

'We were in Barcelona for a week and only got back this afternoon. Manuel was so mysterious on the telephone about why it was necessary for us to be here this evening,' Luis began.

'I asked you all here tonight to share in this most happy occasion. I am sure my brother would have extended the invitation himself, but he has been so busy,' Manuel interrupted with an innocent grin. He carried a large silver tray with glasses of champagne and passed them around with a surprisingly steady hand. When each one had taken a glass, he set the empty tray on a low table and proposed a toast. 'To Joanna,' he said huskily, 'the remarkable woman who has brought life and love back into our home. May she have many fine sons to carry on the proud name of Santiago!'

Joanna stood quivering as they all hid their astonishment and held their glasses up to her, but the dark eyes she sought were cold and harsh and full of grim bleak pain.

After that, the rest of the evening became even more of a nightmare. Josefa had prepared an elaborate Spanish meal, but it could have been sawdust for all Joanna noticed.

Don Rafael sat at the head of the table in thin-lipped silence and Joanna, at his right, tried not to look his way unless it was absolutely necessary. It tore at her heart to see the pain flickering on his face each time he looked at

Elena Vegas. White ridges sprang out at the sides of his mouth as he toyed with his meal.

Elena sat next to Luis Sanchez, across the table from Joanna, and after a while her high artificial laugh began to grate on her nerves. She took a great delight in reminiscing about the good times before Don Rafael retired from the bullring. Once in a while she mentioned her late husband who had died several years before, but anyone could see being a widow didn't upset her in the least.

The others, with the exception of Manuel and Luis Sanchez, politely ignored her and tried to engage in their own desultory conversation at the other end of the table.

'You are not touching your wine, Joanna.' Don Rafael roused himself with a great effort as if he suddenly realised he was neglecting his duties both as host and as expectant bridegroom.

'Perhaps she doesn't care for your Spanish wine, Rafe,' Elena said in her defence. 'California wine is probably more to her liking. After all, our wine is not quite as bitter as this stuff.' She grimaced and picked up her crystal goblet with fragile fingers, their tips immaculately lacquered with a bright red nail polish.

A pain like a knife twisted in Joanna's stomach. 'No, that isn't it at all,' she said softly. 'I can't pretend to be any kind of connoisseur. It's just that I've never really cared for any kind of wine.'

'Well, you're going to find it extremely difficult living in Spain, then. They have wine at all their meals. No self-respecting Spaniard would be without it.' She glanced coyly at Don Rafael. 'Or do you intend to try to civilise Rafe here?' She trilled a harsh grating laugh that sent a chill down Joanna's spine. 'It's something I tried to do for ages and ages, but he wouldn't oblige me in that—but he made up for it in other ways. Right, honey?' A suggestive smile spread over her face as she leaned towards him.

Joanna swallowed and anger finally overcame despair. How could Rafael just sit there and not say anything? Didn't he know how demoralising it was having to listen to this woman make such innuendoes? Something snapped inside her. 'I can't imagine why you'd want to change him in any way, *señora*. Surely when you knew him, he must have been perfect in every way.' She stood up with a jerk and avoided looking at the shocked faces of his guests. 'Please excuse me,' she choked, and practically ran from the room.

'Joanna!' Don Rafael's voice had the harsh ring of command.

She flitted across the hall like a pale green ghost, running up the stairs, willing the tears that threatened to blind her not to fall. That would be the final humiliation. It was obvious she didn't belong with this select gathering. She couldn't even control her temper in front of all Rafael's well bred friends. All evening she had endured the silent censure, but it was impossible to sit there a moment longer.

Isabel Montoya was every inch an aristocrat, sitting at the foot of the table with disapproval written all over her face all evening, and Carlos and Ana Seguras, though kind and seemingly sympathetic, couldn't disguise their objection either. Evidently all of them came from very wealthy noble Spanish families and couldn't understand Don Rafael's sudden infatuation with this girl who had no claim to nobility. It was totally out of character for him. Even Elena Vegas, as a widow of a well-to-do Spaniard, had been accepted here because of her advantageous marriage. But Joanna thought her the most coarse and rude person she had met in a long time. Luis Sanchez was an enigma, but she had no doubt he could claim nobility too.

But not me, she thought wildly. I don't belong here.

That much is painfully obvious. I'm a working girl who came to this house with absolutely nothing, not even decent clothes on my back. I can't compare to his gracious friends. Watching him tonight, she saw just how far apart their worlds really were.

Once she reached the upper hall, her mad flight was stopped in mid-stride when Don Rafael gripped her shoulders and jerked her backward, dragging her against him, close against the hardness of his body. 'You have been extremely rude to our guests,' he said harshly in her ear.

She felt the heat and strength of him through the thin material of her gown, his rapid breath in her hair, his harsh grip on the soft flesh of her shoulders, and she couldn't suppress a shudder. 'They're your guests, not mine. I couldn't sit there any longer. They think you're out of your mind, and they're right. You've got to be crazy to consider going on with this farce. You must see that now? I'd never make a suitable wife for you.'

He twisted her round in his arms, holding her close, and gave her a freezing look that made her quiver. 'The first thing you must learn as *duquesa* is to conduct yourself with proper decorum at all times. No matter how unpleasant the situation, you will respond with dignity and present a gracious and charming front to everyone. You will not run from unpleasantness. You will stand up and face what has to be faced with grace and a certain amount of majesty.' His voice was savage yet at the same time curiously gentle. 'I do not think I am wrong about you, Joanna. When you first came to me, I thought you had courage. It is a rare commodity in a woman, but as my *duquesa* you will be called upon to display that courage.'

'You can't mean to go on with this! You must tell your friends you were tricked into this—this betrothal. They'll understand that a lot easier than if you go through with this farce.'

He turned away abruptly and sought in his pocket for a cheroot. After lighting one, he inhaled deeply and then trailed the fingers of one hand down his cheek as if struggling with himself. 'We must go on, even though I am much different from you, much more experienced and of a different nationality.' His voice became cold with implacability. 'I shall not be made a laughing-stock. If you left me now, I would never live it down. People will question why anyone would choose to tie herself to a disfigured man. No one is to know we were tricked into this union. In fact, it is my command that you tell no one. Let them speculate. In time they will tire of wondering about us and when there is no fuel for the fire of their curiosity, they will turn their attention to more important matters.' He inhaled again and stared at her ashen face through the haze of smoke coming from his lips. 'There is no way you will stop this marriage from taking place at the end of the week, but you do not have to be afraid of me. Ever. I shall ask nothing of you as a wife except that you live here in my home and do nothing to bring disgrace to my name. Do you understand what I am saying?'

A brilliant shade of red swept to her face and she twisted her hands together desperately. 'But what about?—Manuel said——' she stammered, 'You need an—heir—to carry on your name. That's the only reason behind this whole stupid nightmare.'

'It is no longer important.' He flung his cheroot out of a hall window defeatedly. 'I will not force you to become the mother of my children. It is enough that you are forced to become my wife.' He took her elbow and firmly led her to the door of her room. 'I will explain to our guests that you have not yet adjusted to our late hours and convey your apologies. In the future you will see that this does not happen again.'

Joanna knew she should have stood her ground and insisted that this farce be stopped at once, but as she stood looking up at him, she trembled with excitement, apprehension and giddy anticipation all mixed up together. He was stubborn and proud and completely immovable, and she found herself daring to wonder what it would be like married to such a man.

She thought again of that fleeting moment when he had let down his guard and taken her in his arms on the way to Malaga, and the remembered feel of his lips on hers set her trembling all over again. She lifted her chin higher. I love him, she thought, and looked straight into his bleak eyes. He doesn't love me, but I love him, and it's enough. I'll make it enough.

'Very well, Excellency,' she bowed in obeisance, blatantly ignoring his darkening anger at her mocking attempt at servility. 'And Don Rafael?' She risked yet another look at him. 'I will never again give you any cause to be ashamed of me.'

A ghost of a smile flickered across his face. 'I think since we are now officially betrothed you should call me Rafael, no? I remember one morning you had no trouble saying my name.'

'Rafael,' she whispered softly, her face a bright, bright red.

The rest of the evening passed slowly. Confused and restless without understanding why, Joanna went into the bathroom and splashed cold water on her face before changing into a white cotton nightgown. But she was too unsettled to sleep. Now and then she heard the murmur of voices and a shrill laugh that must belong to Elena Vegas and, later, the sound of cars being driven away into the cool, flower-scented darkness. Long after everyone had retired for the night, she sat at her open window staring at the silvery pools of moonlight on the shore in the velvety blackness.

Without her becoming aware of it, the incessant murmur of the sea soothed her, the rhythmic hum of crickets throbbed in her ears and the gentle breeze rustling through the flowering vines somehow eased her restlessness. She dropped her head on her arms at the windowsill and slept.

CHAPTER FIVE

JOANNA woke before the sun was up and through the open window she sensed the sleepy hush that had fallen over the entire length of the valley. Even the breeze had stopped. Only the sea continued its rhythmic motion as if beckoning her to its soothing expanse. She blinked in a dazed fashion and tried to get her bearings.

Last night, just before she fell asleep, she remembered thinking what a strange, unfathomable man Don Rafael was. Through conversation at the dinner table she had found that he had fought bulls because he wanted to make his own name for himself rather than rest on the accomplishments of his ancestors. At that time it was unthinkable for the nobility to do such a thing, but he hadn't cared what people thought. He had become a *matador* in spite of public opinion. And yet now he was letting himself be forced into a marriage because it had been announced in the papers. Now he cared. Why now and not then? It didn't make sense. There had to be something else behind it. Just this once she wished she could understand him.

She was confused and frightened. From the moment she had stepped into his study, she seemed to have relinquished all control over her life. She was no longer a simple ordinary secretary to an up-and-coming executive in New York City. Now she was engaged to a scarred Spanish duke, forced to live in his beautiful country and about to become his duchess. The thought was ludicrous.

She pushed back her hair and stretched from her cramped position at the windowsill. If only she could wake up from this nightmare! None of it made any sense. Maybe if she had more mundane matters to occupy her, she wouldn't feel so threatened or so lost. She resolutely thrust all disquieting thoughts from her mind and rummaged through the closet before she came up with a simple pale blue cotton shift. This morning, at least, was hers and nothing would take it away. She might never again have this chance to be alone without a dour *duena* at her heels.

In practically no time at all she washed and dressed and dragged a brush through her hair. In her bare feet, she quietly went down the stairs and out the front door. The air was cool but heavy with perfume and the grass was covered with dew and tickled her toes as she made her way out of the courtyard, past the high iron gates to a well-worn path that led to the sea, where enchantment gripped her and left no room for any disquieting thoughts.

The sunrise on the beach was dazzling when she finally found a rock large enough to sit on. Her knees were drawn up to her chin and she sat basking in a golden silence, letting the tranquillity pour over her like balm on an open wound. Her eyes never left the gentle waves that lapped the sand as the sun began its ascent. If only time could hang suspended, if only this moment could last, she would be content. Even without the dark brooding duke who was her betrothed, this was the epitome of all her dreams of Spain: the sun and sea and sky in shining blue and gold splendour. She didn't need soul-stirring guitars or fiery *flamenco* to know she was here. This was the best part of Spain and it was hers for the taking.

Suddenly she flung her arms wide and sprang from her huddled position on the rock as if she could not contain the beauty any longer. The water was soothingly warm as it swirled about her toes, and she lifted her arms to the sky in a gesture of homage that was purely impulsive. A warm smile curved her lips and for that brief shining moment, she let a sweet ecstasy sweep over her as she stood ankle-deep in the water. Then her bemused gaze fell on a Moorish tower in the hazy distance and she let her imagination soar. El Cid might have walked along this very shore, defending Spain from the threatened raids of the Moors. She pictured him on his horse, a proud erect figure seated with sinuous grace, his chain mail dully glinting in the first rays of the morning sun.

She blinked her eyes and rubbed them with her fists as a child might. It was crazy! This was supposed to be her imagination, but there was someone coming towards her, galloping hard, across the sand. As he came closer, she recognised the man on the back of his sleek black horse and she stood rooted to the spot, feeling ridiculously like a very young child caught with her fingers in a cookie jar.

Don Rafael was still wearing the same clothes he had worn last night, but his tie was gone and the white silk shirt beneath his dark grey jacket was unfastened almost to his waist. The stubble on his chin and deep shadows under his eyes made it obvious that he was just returning home, and she was surprised at the pang of jealousy that stabbed at her when she thought about where he had spent the night and with whom. Elena must have realised his scars were not so unattractive after all, and her heart twisted painfully.

He stopped several feet away from her and sat easily in the saddle looking down at her with a strange brooding glitter in his eyes. She felt small and embarrassed and hot colour surged to her cheeks, but she remained still while the water gurgled around her ankles. She wouldn't let her eyes waver from his, and suddenly he threw his head back and laughed, and the strangely mournful sound was carried away on the breeze.

'You are such a child, Joanna. If you could see yourself now!' He shook his head and smiled widely as though enjoying a huge joke at her expense.

Her first thought was to bolt and run from this humiliation, but then she remembered his words from last night and decided to try it then and there.

No matter how unpleasant the situation, you will respond with dignity and present a gracious and charming front to everyone.

'Good morning, Rafael. It's a lovely morning, isn't it?'

The smile was abruptly wiped from his face and he shifted in his saddle thunderstruck. This was clearly not the reaction he had expected from her.

She had actually disconcerted him, and she hid her amazement behind a provocative smile. 'This morning promised to be so beautiful and the sea was so inviting, I couldn't resist.' She lifted a graceful foot and trailed her toes in a small arc through the water in front of her. 'Even a *duquesa* is allowed her moments of sheer joy—is she not?'

'So,' he slid from the saddle and stood on the sand at the water's edge, 'you have reconciled yourself to the fact that you and I will be married, have you?'

Joanna lifted her chin. 'Would it do me any good to point out my unsuitability again?'

'Is that what all this is about?' His face suddenly hardened.

She hadn't planned for him to find her this way, but perhaps she could turn it to her advantage and it would show him more clearly than any amount of pleading on her part that she would never make a suitable duchess for him. 'Now how could I possibly know that you would come riding by at just this precise moment and find me here?' she said with all innocence. 'A Spanish wife is supposed to turn a blind eye to her husband's nightly escapades and pretend she doesn't know anything about them, isn't she? I've read about all that hot blood and Latin passion——'

'You will stop this instant!' he commanded. 'What do you know of Spanish temperament? I am just a man, not some stereotypical Spaniard in a book you have read. Your information is grossly unjust to my nationality.' His temper flared and she could feel it across the small distance that separated them.

She took a step backward, deeper into the water, knowing he couldn't follow her because he was fully dressed. Even before he would have time to remove his shoes to come after her, she could run past him and reach the safety of his house—and her *duena*. He wouldn't dare chastise her in front of his disapproving aunt.

Emboldened by the thought, she went on relentlessly: 'What's the matter? Are you ashamed of that aspect of your race? Am I, as a woman, not supposed to know about such things? Latin men must be forgiven much because it's in their blood, isn't that so? They cannot change—or deny—their nature,' she taunted. 'Last night you told me I mustn't do anything to disgrace your name, yet here you are this morning on your way home from a very—eventful—night by the looks of you. But no one is supposed to see that the Duque has been far from discreet,' she accused bitterly.

'That is enough! You will never speak to me like this again. Is that understood?'

Joanna stood her ground defiantly, feeling great courage with the water between them. 'This *duquesa* doesn't like to be ordered about, *señor duque*!'

In an instant he was in the water after her, uncaring that he was ruining his shoes and slacks. She stared in stupefaction and before she could even move, he reached out and dragged her close to him so that her face was only inches away from his.

'Do not ever imply such criticism again! *Dios!* If I did not know better, I would say you are acting like a jealous wife!'

Of course she was jealous. She was going to be his wife and he was coming home from a night spent in the arms of a beautiful woman. Why shouldn't she be jealous? She was more human than he. She had feelings he couldn't even guess at. But he didn't, couldn't know that.

'Let me go!' she snapped, trying to jerk herself free. The movement threw them both off balance and together they sprawled in the shallow water and Joanna sputtered as a small wave splashed in her face. 'Now look what you've done!' She blinked rapidly and tried to wipe her eyes.

'I have done nothing. This is entirely your fault. This time you have tried me too far.'

'My fault? You've ruined your shoes and your suit, yet you're the one who's always in complete control of everything. You never do anything without planning it all out beforehand, do you? You even went so far as to take me to Malaga to make sure you could tell the reporters I was engaged to your brother. But it backfired on you, didn't it? What a waste of time for you! You went all that way and braved all those stares for nothing. It would have been better if you had stayed at home, hiding in the shadows of your study, so no one could see your scars, then Manuel wouldn't have been here to tell the newspaper men that they misunderstood you in the confusion of the moment. Your life would have been all safe and tidy. You could have stayed the recluse with his frightful scar, the *duque* who pretends to have no feelings, who denies all that hot blood . . .' Suddenly her heart began to beat thick in her ears as the look on his face changed to one of terrible anger. This time she had gone too far.

'A recluse? No feelings? Hot blood? What do you know of it?' he muttered savagely, goaded beyond reason. 'I could kill you——' He swung her on to her back and pinned her down in the water, his arms on either side of her, and then with a muffled exclamation his mouth crushed hers in a ruthless, punishing kiss that shook her soul.

The water swirled and eddied about them, but Joanna was lost in an abandonment of feeling that excluded everything else. His cruelty surfaced as his lips ground against hers with insulting thoroughness. His hard fingers tightened on her arms as he crushed her to him and then, as suddenly as it began, the quality of his kiss changed. It became searching and at once her resistance slipped away. She yielded to him with a passion that surprised her. All her unconscious longing surfaced and she realised this was all she wanted, this was what she yearned for. She wanted to press herself even closer to him. She was his. She belonged to him. Long before they ever met, she had been his. Her arms crept up to his neck and when her fingers tangled in his soaked hair, he made no effort to resist her. A wild tremor shook her at the completeness of his response.

Then suddenly he tore himself away from her and stood upright, dragging his hands across his face, pushing his sodden hair out of his eyes. '*Por Dios!*' he groaned. 'What am I doing?' He stood looking at her lying in the shallow water and the glazed look in his eyes made her quiver. He reached down and hauled her out of the water without a word.

Little pools dripped about them as they stood on the

sand, stiff and shaken, looking at each other.

'Rafael——' she began.

'Do not say any more.' He held up his hand. 'I shall not ask you to forgive me. You drove me to this madness. Shall we forget it ever happened?' He turned and, seeing his horse had disappeared, walked swiftly up the path towards his house. It was strange how he could still carry himself with grace and dignity even though his shoes squelched with every step. His suit was plastered to his straight back and rigid shoulders but still his head tilted upwards with the arrogant pride that was so much a part of him.

Joanna felt ashamed. She had driven him too far this time and now there was no way to apologise. A sigh escaped her as she followed behind him. There was nothing she could do now to make it right between them. The best thing to do was to keep out of his way as much as she could.

Isabel Montoya was waiting in the courtyard when they returned. 'Where have you been, Rafael? I have been looking for you. Miss Taylor is not in her room. Her bed has not been slept in.' She stopped suddenly and stared hard as Joanna followed behind him, very much subdued. '*Dios!* What has happened to you both?'

Joanna's dress was clinging wetly to her slender body and her hair hung in dark ropes down her back. A trickle of water dripped down her nose. Don Rafael's clothes were sodden, outlining the muscles in his arms and legs. His hair gleamed in black spikes across his forehead, sprinkled with crystal droplets of water.

'Do not ask,' he said harshly.

Isabel Montoya's eyes narrowed. 'Could you not wait until the end of the week, Rafael? Could you not refuse to sample the wares before the ceremony?'

Joanna's breath caught harshly in her throat.

'That is enough!' he thundered. 'You will apologise to Joanna, Isabel. You do not know anything about it.' He stepped past them, dripping, and disappeared into his house with cold dignity.

'I am sorry, *señorita*,' Isabel Montoya said haughtily. 'I do not like to see my nephew taken for a fool. You have been very unwise. Rafael has a position to maintain and you are no asset to him.'

'No one knows that better than I,' she said softly. 'If you will excuse me, *señora*, I must get out of these wet clothes.' Even though she tried to hold her head high and walk away with poise, she knew she had failed miserably.

Isabel Montoya followed Joanna to her room and waited while she searched in the closet for a robe.

'Surely I'm allowed some privacy, *señora*?' She turned to her. 'I'd like to shower and change instead of dripping all over this carpet.'

'Never before in this noble family has this situation in which you find yourself arisen. You are very foolish, and I cannot see what Rafael sees in you.'

Joanna breathed deeply and counted to ten. 'Have you ever heard the expression, love is blind, *señora*?'

She compressed her lips. 'You cannot convince me that love has anything to do with this union. You are obviously marrying Rafael for his wealth, but why is he marrying you? What have you to offer him?'

A dull red flush crept up her neck. 'I am not marrying Rafael for his money, no matter what you think. Is it so impossible to imagine I love him only for himself?'

'Bah! No young girl would willingly tie herself to a disfigured man if it were not for his wealth. You have your heart set on becoming a *duquesa*. You are greedy for the wealth and the power.' She advanced closer to Joanna standing by the closet. 'But let me tell you, no one will ever take Matilda's place.'

Joanna's eyes widened but she stood still and spoke quietly: 'I'm not so foolish to think anyone could ever take her place. I wouldn't even try. Matilda was Rafael's wife and I'm sure he loved her very much. When he mentions her name, I can see her death still causes him much sorrow. Our marriage will be entirely different from what he had with her.' She gripped her robe tightly in her hands and started for the door. She didn't want Isabel to gloat over the bleakness sure to show in her eyes. Matilda would have given Rafael a son eventually, but Joanna knew there would be no sons for her. She would never be a mother. Because of Rafael's fierce pride they were forced to share a house and a name and a title, but they would never share a life, and certainly there would never be a sharing of love.

But Isabel Montoya was not satisfied to let the matter rest. 'What will you bring to your bridegroom, *señorita*? Matilda had a handsome dowry. She provided Rafael with a villa in Madrid. Such is the Spanish custom, for the bride to bring something of value.'

Joanna stopped in the hallway and turned to face the relentless Isabel. 'That is between Rafael and myself, *señora*.'

'You are coming to him emptyhanded—do not deny it. The clothes you have are not American made. He has provided you with everything, even the most basic necessities. But what are you giving him?'

Joanna struggled with herself. She must maintain a calm front, but it became more and more difficult in the face of this woman's hostility. Her only defence was attack. 'Have you been going through my drawers, *señora*? In my country such a thing is considered quite vulgar.'

Isabel jerked her head back as if she had been slapped, but she straightened her spine and assumed a dignified stance. 'No bride has come emptyhanded to the Santiago family for more than eleven centuries—until now. It is extremely unfortunate that Rafael has stooped so low as to choose a penniless girl who is not even Spanish to become the next *duquesa*.'

'I prefer to think of myself merely as Rafael's wife, not his *duquesa*,' she said coldly, then turned on her heel and closed the bathroom door behind her with a decided slam. Only when she was alone did she put her hands up to her face. This was never going to work. She loved Rafael, but love was not enough. Yet what could she do? She had nothing else to give him. Her eyes blurred, and then she stepped beneath the warm shower to let the water mingle with her tears as if it could wash them away.

The next few days were far from comfortable for Joanna. A staff of servants moved in and turned the place upside down. There were women who helped with the cleaning as well as personal maids for Isabel and herself—a fact Joanna had difficulty in accepting. Don Rafael had also hired two gardeners, a chauffeur and a man to care for his stable of horses. And it seemed to her that she could not walk from one room to another without having to smile courteously at someone.

Dressmakers had come from Barcelona and Madrid to fashion the finest wedding gown of satin and lace, and she was required to stand quite still during the many fittings for long hours under the disapproving stare of her *duena*.

Each morning she forced a polite smile to her pale face and each night in the privacy of her bedroom, she cried herself to sleep.

Don Rafael maintained a polite distance and rarely spoke to her even during the strained meals they shared in the huge formal dining room with Manuel and Isabel. Manuel seemed unusually subdued, but whenever he caught Joanna's puzzled gaze on him, he would smile eagerly and force himself to become animated. She longed to ask him what was wrong, but Isabel's continual presence proved a hindrance to any kind of earnest conversation between them. Even the young girl from the village who served the meals and helped Josefa in the kitchen only added to the tense atmosphere. She tried so hard to please, but Isabel found fault with the service continually and berated the girl in loud harsh Spanish which Joanna couldn't comprehend.

On the night before they were to be married, Don Rafael sat at the head of the table impeccably dressed in a black silk suit, pushing the food restlessly around his plate. His appetite, like hers, had dwindled and he had been in a strange mood all evening. Joanna gave a slight shiver at finding herself pinned by his searching stare. He shoved a hand into his jacket pocket and continued to watch her.

'I have been trying to decide where to take you on our honeymoon, Joanna.' His dispassionate gaze slid over her face and he quirked an eyebrow at her sudden furious blush. 'Is there any special place you would like to visit?'

She fumbled with her fork, trying not to let it clatter against her plate before taking a sip of water. Surely something would happen before tomorrow to prevent their marriage from taking place. Each day she waited for him to come to his senses and tell her that this farce had gone on long enough. He had a fierce stubborn pride, but he must have realised in this past week that it wouldn't work. He had been tense and strained and unusually irritable, not only with the new servants but also with Josefa, and she knew it was because he dreaded this wedding as much as she.

'Well, Joanna?' He sounded impatient, and she gulped.

'There is one place I've always wanted to see,' she said hesitantly. 'It's the embodiment of everything I believe Spain to be.'

'The Alhambra, no doubt.' Isabel Montoya spoke scathingly from the other side of the table. 'Every tourist comes to ooh and ahh over the place and its treasures of art, as if there was nothing else of interest in Granada.'

'But it is very beautiful, Tia,' Manuel said quickly to defend Joanna.

'You would have your brother dragged about Spain as if he were a common tourist?'

'That is enough, both of you!' Don Rafael's voice was quiet, but he clenched his fist on the table, clearly upset at this interruption. 'I have asked Joanna where she would like to go. I do not think she needs any help from either of you to decide on the place she would like to visit.' He turned his dark eyes to her and his mouth twisted in a grimace that could not really be called a smile. 'Well?'

'I'd like to go to Burgos if it's possible,' she said faintly.

'Burgos!' Isabel gasped. 'What in God's name is in Burgos?'

Manuel grinned broadly. 'Do you not know, Tia?'

A flicker of amusement passed over Don Rafael's face. 'My romantic *niña*!' He shook his head. 'It is very cold in northern Spain this time of year. And also very sad, I think.'

'His birthplace is there as well as his tomb,' Joanna said softly. 'I always thought he lived a very sad life, but there were times when he was with his wife and family and I like to think he was happy then.'

Isabel looked a trifle put out and was clearly angry at this conversation she couldn't follow. 'Whose birthplace and tomb? What are you talking about?'

'El Cid, Tia,' Don Rafael said quietly, not taking his eyes from Joanna. 'I should have known my romantic *novia* would be captivated by the medieval knight who defended Spain against her many enemies.'

'So. The Cid is your hero, foolish girl.' Isabel couldn't control her dislike. 'In reality he was an unscrupulous traitor, warlike and ambitious, ruled only by his appetite for wealth and power. He made war on either Moslem or Christian, whichever was advantageous to him at the moment.' Her lips curled in a hateful sneer. 'It is fitting you should admire such a one as he. You are just as greedy. Look at the way you dare to become Duquesa!'

Joanna's fists clenched at her sides and she stood up with a jerk, glaring at the haughty woman across the table. The tense silence filling the room seemed endless, but Joanna managed to hang on to her quivering temper and keep her dignity. After a full minute of struggling for control, she sat back in her chair and slowly let out her breath.

'You will never say such things to Joanna again, Isabel!' White ridges bracketed Don Rafael's mouth and his expression was grim. He spoke with an almost deadly quiet. 'I have chosen her to be my bride and you have no right to criticise that choice.'

'You must be out of your mind, Rafael.'

His eyes took on a bleak, faraway look. 'Do they not say love makes fools of even the wisest men?'

Isabel drew her breath in sharply. 'Do not speak of love,' she said with contempt before coldly stalking out of the room.

Manuel smiled sadly. 'She has always disapproved of everyone and everything.' He shook his head and stood up looking suddenly haggard. 'But I never remembered her being so bitter. Forgive her, Joanna, I am sure she does not mean to be so.' He shrugged expressively and sauntered out of the room, leaving her alone with Don Rafael.

An uncomfortable silence settled between them, stretching like a taut thin wire. Joanna knew she should excuse herself gracefully, but how could she possibly carry it off now? 'Perhaps Burgos wasn't such a good choice after all,' she sighed.

'I was hoping you would want to see Madrid.' Rafael reached in his pocket and calmly withdrew a cheroot. 'Luis Sanchez is fighting there this Sunday and has asked us to be present. It will be his first fight as a full-fledged *matador*.'

'Luis Sanchez is a *matador*?' she gulped in surprise. '*That's* what was too familiar about him! He stands just the way you do.' Her eyes widened when she realised she was speaking her thoughts out loud.

'And how do I stand?' Rafael paused with his lighter half way up to his face.

She twisted her hands in her lap and looked away. 'I'm sorry, I—I spoke without thinking.'

'Come, Joanna. I am soon to be your husband, let there be no secrets between us. Tell me what you mean.'

She swallowed and lifted her face up to him. The flame from his lighter played cruelly over his scar, making it flutter in a grotesque line, and for a moment she thought he held the lighter there purposely, to sustain her awareness of it. 'You always stand with your feet planted firmly as if you're sizing up a bull. There are times when I can almost see the red cape in your hands while you stand so still. It unnerves me.' She shuddered.

He lit the tip of his cheroot and blew the smoke in a thin stream away from the table. 'Tell me, does it bother you that I have been a *matador*? That I have friends who are also in this profession?'

'No, it doesn't bother me,' she said with complete honesty, 'and I really wasn't surprised when Manuel first told me about you. I used to think all Spanish men fought bulls at one time or another and played the guitar and danced flamenco.'

Something flickered in his eyes but was gone in an instant. 'And I always thought all people from America were ill-mannered, selfish and never knew the meaning of the word honesty! It seems we are both guilty of letting our stereotyped notions of another nationality cloud our judgment. Yes?'

Joanna nodded, biting her lip, and then her voice was breathless. 'Does that mean you don't feel the same as Señora Montoya? About me, I mean. You don't still think I'm just a greedy woman out for what I can get from you?'

His enigmatic gaze roamed over the golden hair swept back from her face and lingered on the pale shadows smudged beneath her eyes. She sat still and straight in an evening dress of the palest rose voile, waiting expectantly. Suddenly he leaned towards her, reaching out for her hand. 'Joanna——'

'*Perdoneme, señor!*' The little maid who helped Josefa in the kitchen interrupted them breathlessly before backing away in confusion. 'I thought you had finished.'

Josefa followed quickly behind her and began correcting the girl in a volatile burst of Spanish that rapidly dwindled away as they left the room almost as suddenly as they came.

But the fragile moment between them was shattered like so much splintered glass. Don Rafael rose from the table with his usual dignified grace and turned to her, bowing with the ingrained courtesy that came second nature to him. 'If you have finished, will you come with me to my study?'

'Of course.' On legs that were not quite steady, she preceded him from the room.

The last time she had been in his study, the night he found her searching for her passport, one lamp had been dimly lit, casting vague uncertain shadows to the far corners, and that was the way she always pictured this room, with Don Rafael brooding in the darkness behind his desk, hiding his scarred face away from prying eyes. But this evening she saw that the character of it had completely changed. It was bright and warm and even cozy. The heavy dark red curtains that usually covered the windows had been drawn back to expose the gleaming glass with the silvery glints of moonlight in the darkness of the garden beyond them. A small fire was burning in the fireplace at one side of the room to dispel the dampness and this, along with several lamps flickering in wall sconces, chased away the chilly gloom considerably.

She turned to him with surprised approval shining in her eyes.

He bowed slightly as if in acknowledgment and glanced around the room before moving behind his desk. 'You dared to accuse me of hiding in the shadows of this room,' he said conversationally, but bitterness tinged his voice and his hand moved along the puckered edge of his scar.

She twisted her hands together, turning rigidly away from the pain in his eyes, remembering the accusation she flung at him and the flush that suddenly stained her cheeks almost matched the rose colour of her dress. 'I had no right to say what I did that day.'

'You said what you thought was the truth.'

'I was angry.'

'It is of no matter. Sometimes anger forces us to face a truth we are afraid to see.' His fingers left his mangled cheek and with jerky movements that were not at all like him, he opened his desk drawer and withdrew a small grey-blue booklet. The gold lettering on the cover glinted dully in the light and Joanna stared at it as if mesmerised.

He slid it across the smooth polished surface of his desk. 'Take it, Joanna. You will have need of it.'

She drew in a shaky breath but did not move to touch

it. 'Are you telling me this passport wasn't counterfeit after all? You lied to me?'

His expression hardened almost to a sneer. 'It was the poorest of imitations, a very shoddy "official" document. But I have—how do you say?—pulled some strings and now you should have no trouble travelling wherever you wish to go. Take it!' he commanded harshly before turning away from her to stare out broodingly at the velvety blackness of the night.

For a moment she stood motionless, oddly hurt by his cold remoteness. She didn't know what to think, but sudden fragments of hope and dismay chased each other through her mind. By giving her this passport tonight, before their wedding, he was, in effect, offering her her freedom. She didn't have to marry him. It's for the best and this is what I want, a small insistent voice echoed in the back of her mind. This is what I've been waiting for all week. He doesn't need to say it. His actions are louder than any words could be. He's telling me I'm free to leave. There's nothing to stop me now. I can leave this evening and no one will stop me. He's giving it to me because he doesn't want me to stay. He could never love me. I'm a child to him and he can't marry a child. Hurt pride dimmed her eyes.

She forced her nerveless limbs to action, reaching out to pick up the document from the desk. Her trembling hands turned it over and over, but her numbed gaze roamed over the shape of his arrogant head to his broad shoulders and then to the whole lean length of him. Fine threads of silver glinted through his hair in the flickering firelight, but it would be a long time before the thick blackness was totally taken over by age and she would not be here to see it.

Somehow she couldn't imagine him as an old man, stooped and withered and alone. Power was in every inch of his long lean body, a power that made him refuse to be at the mercy of mere human elements. He would refuse to age just as he was refusing to marry her. He could never allow anything to happen that he didn't want to happen. She should have remembered that. His pride kept him silent when their betrothal was announced, but that same immense pride stopped him from going through with the actual ceremony. He was letting her go now, allowing her to slip away in the night without facing any recriminations. He would probably issue some kind of formal statement to the press in the morning and bear the brunt of the curiosity and conjecture about them with poise and grace and a certain aloof detachment uniquely his own.

'Thank you,' she whispered, letting her breath out slowly. Then she turned and quietly walked out of the study.

Rafael pressed his hands savagely on the windowsill and continued to stare at the blackness outside without uttering a sound.

Moving like an automaton, Joanna found her way upstairs to her empty bedroom and went in. She sat down on the edge of the bed, shivering. Then her restless footsteps carried her to the window, where she stood listening to the murmur of the sea and then began to cry very quietly.

There was absolutely no reason at all why she should feel so desolate. I'm free to go, she chided herself, and tried to ignore the raw pain that ripped her heart. In the back of my mind I knew he would do something, I knew we wouldn't have to go through with it. Marriage to a man like Rafael is too preposterous. He's a duke and I'm a penniless girl with delusions of grandeur. It's my misfortune I let myself fall in love with him when all along I knew it would never work. He's nothing like me. He knows so much and has experienced things I can only imagine. My mentor, she thought sadly. He could have taught me so many things, but the only thing I really want to know is what it feels like to be loved, really truly loved, by him. The tears coursed silently down her cheeks until the moonlight on the waves became a sodden blur.

It could have been minutes or perhaps even hours that she stood like that. She never knew, because time had ceased to mean anything to her. The tears had long since dried on her face and the moon was high and everything was strangely still when a muffled pounding penetrated her numbed consciousness. She moved to the door on stiff legs and opened it to find Josefa in the hallway staring at her, strangely breathless.

'Oh good, *señorita*, you have not yet changed into your nightclothes. Please come. You must help Don Rafael!'

Her face drained of colour. 'What's happened to him?'

Josefa shook her head. 'Doña Elena has come. Please, *señorita*, you must not let him be hurt again.'

'Doña Elena?' Joanna stopped her mad flight in the middle of the stairway. 'She's here? Now? With Rafael?'

'*Si.*' Josefa's eyes filled with stricken tears. 'I did not mean to listen, but the study door was open and their voices carried.' She wiped her eyes with a handkerchief. 'She said she did not believe you will marry him tomorrow—because of his face. She said it was all a lie for her benefit, to make her jealous. He was only trying to save his pride that she had hurt and you went along with the joke but did not mean to carry it through. Please, *señorita*, she means to make mischief. You must help him! If you care for him at all, you will go to him now and let her see that his scars do not sicken you.' She wrung her hands in desperation. 'Only you can prove to Doña Elena that she no longer has the power to hurt him. She will not believe he has found someone to love him as he is. Please?'

Joanna hesitated. 'But, Josefa, he loves her even though

she hurt him. He doesn't want to marry me.'

'Do not believe it! I heard him tell Doña Elena that you had chosen freely and this was no joke. No one was forcing you to become his wife. He told her to wait and see what happened tomorrow. Do you know what she did? She laughed in his face. She called him a fool and told him he would be left standing at the altar, and she said she would gladly see him suffer before she would pick up the pieces you left behind.'

'No!'

Josefa bent and picked up the blue booklet lying on the stair, her eyes widening in shock. 'Your passport?'

Joanna nodded in a daze. 'I must have dropped it and not realised it. Rafael gave it to me earlier this evening.'

'So that is what he meant when he said you had a choice whether to marry him or not,' she whispered shrewdly. 'And have you chosen?'

Joanna's throat felt dry and tight. 'I only want what's best for him.'

'You are best for him. You said you love him! If you really do, you will not let him be hurt. All week there have been reports in all the newspapers of the coming wedding. They have retraced his family and have made much of his noble ancestors from previous centuries. People are coming from all over Spain to offer him best wishes. Celebrations of many kinds have been planned. You must not leave him now. Do you know what that would do to his pride?'

Joanna wrung her hands. 'But he said nothing—I had no idea.'

'*Señorita*, you love him. You must let him keep his pride.' She thrust the passport into Joanna's hands and nearly pushed her down the rest of the stairs.

Raised voices echoed in the hallway and Joanna stood motionless, listening to the shrill tones of Elena Vegas.

'... you loved me once, I know you did,' she was saying. 'You still love me if only you will admit it. I won't believe this other girl means anything to you. She's just a child!'

'Joanna is more of a woman than you could ever hope to be.' The deep voice was curiously cold.

'You're only saying that to make me jealous. I lowered myself to come here tonight. I should have waited until tomorrow. You'll be looking for consolation then, but you may not get it.'

'Now, *señorita*!' Josefa hissed, pushing Joanna into the doorway of the study. 'You must help him.'

Joanna tried to control her ragged breathing, closing her eyes to the sight of the voluptuous woman dressed in a startling black backless dress, intimately moulded against Rafael's long lean body. His hands were resting on her shoulders, whether to draw her closer or push her away, she couldn't be sure.

'There you are, Rafael,' she said coolly as if she was not aware of having interrupted such an intimate clinch.

He turned to the doorway, dropping his hands to his sides, suddenly defeated, and stepped away from Elena. The familiar look of pain was etched about his mouth, but she smiled brilliantly and hoped he wouldn't notice her trembling as she made her way to him.

'I didn't realise you had company. Hello, *señora*. I imagine you came to wish us well.' She extended her hand to Elena and was not surprised when the other woman refused to acknowledge it.

'I came to speak to Rafe privately,' she retorted spitefully.

'Oh, I see. Forgive me for interrupting, then,' she said smoothly with a dignity that astounded her. She turned to Don Rafael. 'I only came to give you this.' She held out her passport with amazingly steady hands. 'Will you keep it in a safe place for me? With all the confusion that's bound to come before the ceremony tomorrow, I wouldn't want it to get lost.'

He searched her face intently for a moment, then looked down at the passport in her hand. His jaw became taut and she saw a muscle twitch in his cheek, but he said nothing and took the passport from her.

Without pausing to question the wisdom of her impulsive action, she stood on tiptoes. 'Goodnight, my love,' she said clearly before pressing her lips against the livid scar that snaked its way down his cheek.

She felt him flinch, but before she could draw away from him, he reached out and dropped his arm in a possessive trembling grip across her shoulders and ran his fingers over the silky golden tangle of her hair. 'I know you must be tired, *querida*,' his voice was incredibly deep and husky, 'but I find it very difficult to let you go just now.'

'Ah, but after tonight we need never be parted again. Not even for a moment, my darling.'

She heard the swift intake of his breath and her knees went weak. How dare she overstep herself like this?

Elena's face contorted with suppressed rage. 'I seem to be a fifth wheel just now.' Her mouth twisted bitterly, 'I never would have believed it if I hadn't seen it for myself. I always thought you were more discerning, Rafe. But I wish you joy of her. If you ever get tired of this child and want a real woman, you know where to find me.' She tossed her head back haughtily. 'Don't bother to see me to the door. I know the way—too well!'

All of a sudden it became too much for Joanna, and all the life seemed to drain from her as she watched Elena Vegas stalk out of the room, but Rafael tightened his arm about her shoulders, pulling her closer to his twisted angry face.

'Why did you do it, Joanna?' he hissed between his teeth. 'I did not need your assistance with her. You are free to leave.'

'Is that what you want?' Her eyes locked with his.

'It does not matter what I want.'

'But how would you explain my absence to your people tomorrow? Would you really let them think I left you at the altar?'

His face darkened. 'It is what you intended all along, is it not? Did you not ask Josefa for help? Is that not why you were searching in my desk for your passport? You knew before I did what Manuel had accomplished and you tried to run away. I cannot change what he did, but I can give you the opportunity to choose what you want. You will not be forced to marry me merely to save my pride.'

She twisted in his grasp, but he refused to release her. His fingers tightened, digging into her shoulders, making her aware of his sudden trembling. 'I made my choice, Rafael. You don't have a monopoly on pride. If I left you now, I would be branding myself as a coward. There would be no wedding ceremony for all your people who are looking forward to it tomorrow. But I have chosen to stay with you, as your bride, to keep you from being made a laughing-stock. I couldn't leave you to face that blow to your pride alone.' She turned her face away from him, feeling the hot tears pricking the backs of her eyes. He must not see her cry. He wouldn't understand. She looked up at him, aware of him with every fibre of her being. His jaw was taut and lifted to an arrogant angle, and once again she thought he was the most attractive disturbing man she had ever met and all her love for him came welling up. He was so cool, so detached, so very much in command. She wanted to shock him, just once, into an awareness of her.

As her hand began to stroke his scarred cheek, he knocked it away with loathing.

'The charade is over, Joanna,' he said harshly. 'We no longer have an audience, so you need not pretend this scar is not repulsive to you. *Dios*, you are a superb actress! Tell me, how did you keep yourself from shuddering when your soft lips came into contact with this gruesome——'

'Oh, don't!' she cried. 'That scar is not gruesome.' She wrenched herself out of his arms and put the width of his desk between them, staring at him helplessly. Her breath came in short ragged gasps as she bent forward with her fists clenched at her sides. 'What would you hide behind if you didn't have that scar? You seem to think it gives you the right to deny yourself normal human feelings. For the last time, I don't find your face repulsive! I've never met anyone who was more of a man than you are, and I think that scar merely adds to your distinction. You should wear it proudly instead of being ashamed of it. Such a mark shows that you weren't afraid to face the ultimate test of a man's courage!'

Without waiting to witness the explosive anger she knew he was barely controlling, she turned abruptly on her heel and ran from the room, nearly knocking Josefa down as she made her way into the hall.

'*Señorita*, you are wonderful!' Josefa quickly followed her up the stairs. 'You are making him see so many things he has not wanted to see.'

'Please, Josefa,' Joanna took a deep breath, shaken by the depth of her emotions, 'I don't think I can stand any more tonight.'

But she was not allowed the respite. No sooner had she closed the door to her bedroom, leaving Josefa muttering in the hall, than Rafael burst in on her without warning.

'You dare to speak to me like that?'

'Oh, I dare a great deal, *duque*!'

'Do not fling that title at me with such loathing!'

She turned quickly away and crossed the room with barely controlled anger. Her hands twisted tightly in front of her as she stared out the window. 'I can't help it. You're always so correct and dignified all the time, lording it over everybody, not letting anybody forget for one minute you're Spanish royalty. I wish just once you could be an ordinary man.'

'I am an ordinary man, Joanna.'

'No, you're not. Ordinary men have feelings, but you won't allow yourself to have any. You keep everything locked up inside you where nobody can reach you.' She turned and uttered a surprised exclamation. He had come to stand close behind her, but she hadn't heard his soft footsteps and was not prepared for his nearness.

In the soft lamplight he glared down into her startled eyes, his own glittering harshly. 'I am an ordinary man who has been hurt.' Tortured fingers travelled over his scarred cheek. 'When I was gored by the bull, my flesh was torn, but then my body formed scar tissue both tougher and thicker than the original flesh as a protective shell against another injury in the same place. So, too, my feelings. I have a heart, but it is protected from further injury. It is the utmost stupidity for a man to trust a woman with his heart.'

'I would never hurt you, Rafael. Not intentionally.' Her pulse raced alarmingly at the intent look in his tormented eyes. Didn't he know she loved him too much to ever willingly hurt him?

His fingers curled on her arms, drawing her even closer to him. 'You will never have that chance,' he said coldly, 'so you can keep your pity. I do not want it. If you marry me tomorrow it is with the understanding that it is for ever. We do not have flexible divorce laws in this country. It will be a Catholic ceremony conducted in the village church with many people in attendance, from the poorest *peon* to the wealthiest aristocrat. They will expect to see a radiant bride who has accepted me for what I am. Do you think you can do this? Can you marry me, knowing you will possess my name and my wealth but you will never possess my heart?'

Joanna shuddered. His silver-flecked hair lay thick and smooth against his head. His long black lashes darkly framed his eyes, hiding the expression in them. All she wanted was his heart. He could keep his title and his wealth; she only wanted the man beneath the brooding exterior. 'Is there no one you can love? Ever? No one at all?'

He studied her intently. 'No, Joanna. The man who lets himself love a woman is a fool.'

She bent her head, trying to control an unreasoning anger. 'This is wrong. People marry for love, not for any other reason. How can a marriage last without it?' Her tortured eyes met his remote gaze and she could feel him withdrawing from her even though he hadn't moved. She loved him enough for both of them. It had to be enough. Her lips quivered but the words she whispered were clear. 'I intend to become your wife tomorrow.'

'My *duquesa*,' he corrected with a tightened jaw.

'Of course.' She bent her head. He would not let her be his wife, not in the real sense of the word. But she would be his *duquesa*, his ornament, his royal possession.

He released her then and left the room without another word.

Joanna watched the door close silently behind him. Suddenly her legs were too weak to support her and she leaned back against the wall to control their trembling. She breathed deeply to fill her lungs. 'What have I done?' she whispered, pressing her hands to her cheeks. 'Oh, what have I done?'

CHAPTER SIX

EARLY the next morning, Joanna was awakened by the joyful pealing of church bells from the little church in the village. Exhaustion had finally played its part last night and she had slept dreamlessly, but this morning she was wide awake and painfully aware that this was her wedding day. She was going to become the wife of an important Spanish nobleman. Not his wife, she told herself, his *duquesa*. There was a difference. She would have his name, his title and his wealth, but she would never possess the heart of the man she loved.

She dragged herself out of bed, padding to the windows, flinging them wide to the fragrant sunshine and the murmuring sea. I'm here, I've made my choice and I'll make the best of it, she told herself, determined to ignore this awful feeling of emptiness inside her.

Her chin was cupped in her hands and she was still seated at the window when Josefa came with a breakfast tray.

'*Buenos dias, señorita*. I have come today to help you. I thought you would prefer my help to that of the silly Brigida.' Her dark eyes sparkled in her wizened face. 'As a maid, she has much to learn.'

'Brigida means well, but I'm accustomed to doing things for myself. Sometimes she doesn't understand my English.'

'It will come in time. Very soon you will take this way of life for granted and realise she considers it an honour to be your maid and do things for you.'

Joanna turned away from the windows and nervously twisted her hands together. 'Oh, Josefa, I'm so afraid!'

The little woman gave her an understanding smile. 'Every young girl is afraid on her wedding day—it is only natural. But Don Rafael is a good man. He will take care of you and be a gentle and considerate lover. Do not worry.'

Joanna turned abruptly away. 'That's not what I mean. How can I dare to marry a man like him? He's a duke—so far above me.'

'He is just a man, more unhappy than most, with many regrets, but still just a man. I will tell you something, *señorita*, because you are like a daughter to me.' Josefa set the tray on a low table and crossed the room to stand in front of her, taking both her hands firmly. 'Don Rafael has never had anyone to love him. His mother died when Manuel was born. He was only ten at the time. His father was a good man, but he was too obsessed with being a nobleman and too busy adding to the legacy that was to pass to his heirs to spend time with a lonely little boy. So he learned at an early age to disguise his feelings and become self-sufficient. I loved that little boy,' her eyes misted, 'but I am just a servant and it was not my place to show my affection. I could only be kind to him and serve him well. He grew to be a man and I saw him marry a woman who was chosen for him, a woman who did not love him. And then I saw another woman who was not worthy to wipe his shoes spurn his love when he was close to death.

'But you are different, *señorita*. You can give him something he has never had. You can love him as he has never been loved. Even though he has noble titles, he is an ordinary man who has learned to hide his grief and not expect too much out of life. Your love will heal all the hurt he has suffered.'

Joanna's eyes closed on the swift stab of compassion that struck her. Then, impulsively, she hugged Josefa.

'Oh, I hope you're right! Thank you for being such a help to me.'

Josefa blinked rapidly and sniffed. 'Come, you must eat now. Before I forget, Don Rafael said to tell you he will respect the custom of not seeing the bride before the wedding. He will see you in church. But he has asked me to give you this now.'

A small jeweller's box was on the tray beside the coffee pot. When Joanna flicked it open with trembling fingers, an exquisite tear-shaped diamond suspended on a delicate gold chain winked up at her from its bed of blue velvet.

'Josefa!' She looked stricken. 'How can I accept this? It must have cost a small fortune! I've nothing to give him.'

'How can you say this, *señorita*? You are giving him something beyond price. You are giving him your heart. No one else has ever done this. He will find his happiness with you, and for the first time in his life, he will have love. That is something all the money in the world cannot buy. Think about it,' she smiled. 'When you have finished your breakfast, I will return with Doña Isabel to help you get dressed.' The door closed behind her, leaving Joanna standing alone in the middle of the bright beautiful room.

Her wedding dress was deceptively simple. The neckline was high around her throat with a long row of tiny white satin buttons holding it together at the back. Made of the finest delicate lace, it followed the slender curves of her figure before flowing out in a long train behind her. The sleeves were a short cap of lace and she was to wear long white gloves that came above her elbows.

She stood stiffly, letting Josefa pin the *peineta*, the high Spanish comb, into her hair, then bent forward as she lifted the white lace *mantilla* that matched her dress over her head. Its delicate folds were arranged carefully before Josefa fastened it at the back with a brooch of diamonds.

The heavy satin underslip rustled softly when Joanna

moved towards the mirror to stare at the stranger reflected there. Her bright golden hair had been swept back in a loose knot at the base of her neck and was, for the most part, concealed by the *mantilla*. The smooth contours of her face were as pale as alabaster, but her eyes glowed a brilliant blue with all the love she couldn't conceal.

'Your colouring is all wrong for Spanish dress, Miss Taylor,' Isabel said with a disapproving frown. 'That *mantilla*, especially, is wrong. You should have worn something more suitable to you.'

'Josefa told me this is the same *mantilla* Rafael's mother was married in and he wished me to wear it today. I realise light hair doesn't do it justice, but if it will make him happy . . .' Joanna shrugged her shoulders as if to say it really made no difference to her. There was no way she was going to let Isabel take away the thrill of wearing something that belonged to Rafael's mother. She hugged the thought to her.

Isabel tossed her head and smoothed the black silk dress that followed her own tall figure faithfully. 'Matilda was a radiant bride. Her dark colouring complemented her white gown and she wore flowers in her hair instead of the traditional *mantilla*. She played the part of *duquesa* with a certain flair you cannot hope to match. Her glowing black hair had a sheen that made a man want to tangle his fingers in it. Can you say the same of yours, Miss Taylor? You are so pale and lifeless. You do not make half so striking a bride as Matilda did.'

Joanna swallowed her annoyance and lifted her chin. 'Yes, I am different from your godchild, *señora*, in looks as well as temperament. When Rafael looks at me, he will not be reminded of Matilda in any way. That should be a consolation to you.'

Isabel looked as though she had been struck, but then she tossed her head angrily. 'Shall we go?'

Joanna straightened her shoulders, trying to force a look of confidence to her face. 'I haven't forgotten anything, Josefa?'

'Only this,' she said, picking up the diamond necklace from her dressing table. 'Don Rafael expects you to wear it today.'

'Diamonds for you? With Matilda it was rubies. Diamonds are so cold, but rubies are alive with the fire that flows in our blood,' Isabel taunted.

Joanna tried to fasten the necklace, but her fingers shook so badly Josefa had to do it for her.

Isabel stood stiffly by the door, a look of murderous jealousy marring her dark face. 'He has given you so much and you have nothing to give him in return.'

'You're wrong, *señora*,' Joanna said with quiet dignity. 'I'm giving him something priceless.' She swept out of the room without another word and went down the long grilled gallery to meet Manuel at the bottom of the stairs.

He stood tall and handsome in a black suit and gleaming white ruffled shirt. The look in his glowing eyes did everything to bolster her confidence. '*Madre de Dios!* I have never seen anyone more beautiful.' He reached out and took her hands in his at the bottom stair and looked directly into her eyes. 'You will make my brother live and be happy again. I know this!' He pressed an ardent kiss to her hand, then straightened and allowed her to walk past him into the courtyard.

Isabel swept down the stairs behind her and threw him the most contemptuous stare before joining Joanna outside.

The ride to the village church was uncomfortable for all of them. Joanna sat in front with Manuel, and although he did his best to avoid the deep ruts in the road, he seemed to hit most of them. Isabel and Josefa were severely jostled in the back seat and no matter how many times Manuel apologised, Isabel took it as a personal affront to herself.

'Please, Manuel! I know you can drive better than this. Anyone would think this was your weddding day. What are you so nervous about?' She was thrown against Josefa as he hit another pothole.

'We are almost there, *tia*,' he said apologetically, then he turned to grin slightly at Joanna.

Her lips twitched, but she said nothing.

The road leading to the village church was crowded with people who could not find an empty seat inside, and then a sudden silence settled over them when they caught sight of the car. When Joanna stepped out, she heard several gasps, then the general murmur of admiration that ran through the crowd before Manuel gripped her gloved fingers hard.

'It is unusual for a *duque* to marry someone of a different nationality, but these people will have no trouble accepting you. You are fair-skinned and beautiful, and they will come to accept that it is no longer strange. You will see this. Goodbye, Joanna. Make my brother happy!' he said savagely. Then he was gone, leaving her to stare after him as he pushed his way into the church.

She turned with a questioning frown to Josefa standing behind her, but Josefa smiled a bright white smile and motioned for her to go into the church where Rafael was waiting for her.

She had never been in this church before, but at once she liked the whitewashed walls and the many carved statues looking down from their niches as if in reassurance. Riotous flowers had been fastened to the ends of the low wooden pews running the length of the church, and when she stepped forward on to a long white carpet, an organ wheezed to life. She held her head high and gripped a perfect white orchid Rafael had provided for her and made her way down the aisle to him.

He was standing at the altar with his broad back to her, and at the first sound of the organ, he turned slowly to meet her bright blue gaze. He was dressed in formal black with a broad white and gold ribbon fastened over his right shoulder and his chest was covered with medals, but Joanna only saw his dark brooding eyes as they met and clung to hers. His face could have been carved like one of the statues that surrounded them, for he stood unblinking, expressionless, watching her come to him.

She continued to look at him and her heart swelled, bursting into a flame of love that threatened to consume her. She saw no one else as she glided down the aisle. She did not know Elena Vegas sat in the front pew avidly determined to see him hurt again. She saw only Rafael.

Then she was beside him, her cold hand linked with his as they made their vows. His voice was cold and distinct when he repeated the words after the priest, his firm hands steady when he placed the wide gold band on her finger.

She was nervous and pale and her voice shook when she spoke her vows. Her hands trembled so much she almost dropped the broad masculine ring when she took it from the priest before slipping it on to her husband's finger.

Father Esteban clasped their hands together with his and smiled warmly before turning away to finish the Nuptial Mass. Joanna turned her white face to Rafael in mute appeal for some reassurance that he did not totally despise her, but all she saw was the hard taut angle of his jaw with its thick ugly white streak puckering the skin on his arrogant face.

When the Mass was over, they turned to each other in the waiting silence that suddenly fell over all the people crowded in the little church. They looked long into each other's eyes, then Rafael slid his arm around her waist, holding her firmly against him before bending his dark head towards her.

She felt the warmth and strength and power in him flow through her and she lifted her face willingly to receive his kiss of duty. His lips were cool as they brushed against hers in a fleeting kiss before he turned his face away, but she was undaunted by his remoteness. She pressed her lips to his scar and for a shocked moment he stiffened, but he hid his sudden anger with rigid control. She heard an approving murmur filter through the church before the organ once again wheezed to play the recessional.

Then they were out in the sunshine surrounded by a noisy excited crush of dark-haired, dark-skinned people who came to offer their congratulations. Joanna was introduced to many powerful dignitaries, heads of state and wealthy businessmen who had come from far away Spanish cities. She smiled politely, and never before had she had her hand kissed so gallantly by so many.

Making their way to the waiting car, Rafael gripped her elbow to lead her through the crowd. She was touched by the way the simple people removed their hats and bowed graciously as she passed. But before she reached the car, a little girl, perhaps seven years old, dressed in a ragged but clean white dress, pushed her way through the crowd and held out a small bunch of wilted white flowers to her.

'*Muchas gracias, niña.*' Joanna bent down and smiled at the barefoot little girl. She took the flowers and held them to her nose and breathed in their fragrance, then on impulse gave her orchid to the girl.

'Beautiful duchess,' the girl breathed shyly before planting a hasty kiss on her cheek and disappearing back into the crowd.

She straightened and raised her sparkling eyes to her husband, but he averted his head and all she could see was the harsh white ridge that sprang out at the side of his mouth.

He bowed, coldly polite, to the people closest to him, then helped Joanna into the car with frigid courtesy before threading their way back to their home.

There was a distinct invisible barrier between them, but Joanna said nothing. She wouldn't let anything spoil this day for her. This was her wedding day and she had married the man she loved. There would be no regrets now. It was to be a day she would remember for the rest of her life. Through the lowered window beside her, she caught the rich earthy scent of fields and flowers and sunshine mingling with the gentle murmur of the sea. Spain is mine now, she thought, and smiled widely, burying her face in the bedraggled white flowers. It was the first gift she had received that day that had been given with love. The orchid, like the diamond necklace, had been given out of a sense of duty because it was expected of a *duque*. But these simple white flowers, plucked from the Spanish hillside, had been offered with love.

'When we arrive home there will be many of my friends and business acquaintances waiting for us and there will be a formal dinner tonight that will last quite a bit longer than usual.' Rafael spoke abruptly, cutting into her thoughts. 'You have conducted yourself well up to now. I hope you will continue to do so.'

'Of course. You won't have any cause to be ashamed of me.' She saw his mouth compress and his eyes harden as he negotiated the rutted road ahead of them.

Once he hit a deep pothole and she was thrown against him, and for an instant she felt the tingling awareness of his hard body and felt him tremble before she straightened in her seat. He was not as impervious to her as he pretended, and somehow it was that thought alone that helped her get through the rest of the day.

As the hours dragged by, she assumed the position of hostess with polite dignity and grace. Rafael's manner was distant and cold, although he was the gracious host with impeccable manners to all the other guests. Joanna remained by his side and acted the part of the happy bride who basked in the radiant love of her husband.

A large buffet was set up with a mixture of every imaginable canapé and cocktail snack from fruit to meat to fish. Champagne flowed like water.

The guests filled the elegant *sala* and overflowed into bright chattering groups in the glowing garden. Joanna watched them all and kept a charming smile glued to her face.

At one point, when her poise began to slip, she excused herself graciously, making her way to her room to be alone for a few minutes. Rafael was deep in conversation with several men connected with bullfights, and as they discussed the pros and cons of the art, she thought he would not notice her absence.

But she hadn't realised Elena Vegas would follow her up the winding staircase straight to her room.

'So,' Elena said contemptuously, slamming the door behind her, 'you've gone and married the duke after all.'

Joanna whirled around. 'If you please, *señora*. I wish to be alone for a few minutes.'

'Alone?' Elena's face twisted in a hateful sneer. 'So you can cut the gracious duchess act? It's beginning to wear a little thin, isn't it? I've been watching you all day. Rafe hasn't said a word to you other than what was expected of him. It's almost as if he loathes the very sight of you. What's with you two anyway? He certainly doesn't act like an eager groom who can't wait to be alone with his new bride. And now you're up here all by yourself with your face as white as a sheet. What's the matter? Are you having second thoughts already? Are you worried about what it's going to be like when you find yourself in his arms tonight and he presses his scarred body against yours?'

'That's enough!'

'Oh no, it's not. He's shown you his other scars, hasn't he? What did you think of the hideous job those Spanish doctors who call themselves surgeons did on his chest and back? His face is bad enough, but how can you bear to touch that mangled body?'

Joanna felt her face burn with angry colour, but she managed to keep her features composed. Only her hands betrayed her anguish as she bunched them into fists. 'Get out of this room, Elena. I'm forced to be polite to you today because you're my husband's guest. But if you don't leave me alone, I'll show you another side of me that's not polite at all!'

'So it is all an act! I thought so. You're not as cool as you'd like people to think. That was a touching little scene in church today, but a little overdone, don't you think? Whose benefit was it for? Yours or Rafe's? His scars are ugly, but he's a man underneath them, and marriage to a child isn't going to satisfy him for long. Now that he's quit sulking and back in public, he'll come back to me within the month. He always does—just wait and see.'

'What makes you think he doesn't already know how much satisfaction he can have with me?' Joanna said calmly, refusing to let Elena see how much she was upsetting her, how each word she uttered slashed her heart to ribbons.

Elena's breath caught at the back of her throat. 'I don't believe you! Rafe likes his women with flesh on their bones.' She ran a hand along her own voluptuous curves outlined in flame satin. 'A pale skinny creature like you wouldn't appeal to him. You're a child, not a woman.'

Joanna gave her a cold smile. 'You don't know my

husband as well as you think. After all, he married me, didn't he?'

Elena flushed an unbecoming red and her dark eyes suddenly filled with rage. She advanced closer to Joanna and raised a hand in fury to strike her.

Joanna stood her ground without shrinking, and at that moment Rafael walked into the room. His eyes hardened when he saw Elena, but he fixed his cold stare on Joanna.

'Why are you in this room, Joanna? This is no longer where you will stay. Your things have been moved to the room connecting mine.'

She blinked and flushed with sudden triumph as he played right into her hands. 'Do you mean the one I used before you had Señora Montoya come here to act the proper chaperone?' she asked with feigned innocence.

Elena looked at Rafael with hatred and Joanna knew the question had totally shattered her.

'Yes,' he said coldly, 'that one.'

She leaned towards him very slowly, ignoring the harsh frown moving over his face. 'I shouldn't have forgotten. I've been looking forward to occupying it again ever since that first night . . .' She let her voice trail away in a seductive whisper.

Elena breathed in harshly. 'You swine, Rafe!' An obscenity split the air before she slammed her way out the door.

All the colour drained from Joanna's face and she swayed dizzily before Rafael caught her arms, holding her away from him.

'What was that all about?'

She shook her head to clear it. 'I don't think Elena will bother me any more now.' She tried to turn away from him, but he wouldn't release her.

'What was so important you had to leave our other guests to speak to her up here?'

'She followed me—I didn't ask her to come. We were having a discussion about how soon you'll grow tired of me.' She laughed a little harshly. 'That's really funny, isn't it? There won't be anything for you to get tired of.' Her eyes swung up to his and once again she saw the cold bleak pain that was always there when Elena was around. 'Will you promise me one thing, Rafael?'

'What is it?'

'When you do go back to her, you won't let her talk about me.'

'You stupid child,' he said harshly. 'You have so much to learn about men.'

'Will I have you to teach me?'

He frowned, searching her pale face beneath his mother's white lace *mantilla*. Her eyes were brilliantly blue but infinitely sad. Then two bright tears hovered in her eyes before spilling on to her cheeks. 'Tears? On our wedding day?' he jeered. 'It is a bad omen, and you must know how superstitious we Latins are. Come, you must put on a joyful face for our guests. You must act the happy bride in love with her new husband. You have done so well up to now. Certainly you can carry the act a little longer?'

'It's not an act, Rafael,' she said, unable to keep silent. All her love stood out in her eyes. If only he could see it and love her in return!

His face twisted and his fingers dug into her shoulders with punishing strength. 'Do not say any more. I could not stand the lie.'

'Is it so hard to believe I love you?'

'We have been tricked into this marriage and we must make the best of it. Do not make it more difficult by pretending to love me.'

'I chose to marry you, remember?'

'It was not a free choice—we both know that. You mistake pity for love.'

'I didn't marry you out of pity, Rafael. That's the one thing you don't need from anybody. You have enough of your own.'

'How can you say that?' His jaw clenched and his hands fell lifelessly to his sides. 'Do you not realise what I have tried to do for you? I was not thinking of myself when I arranged this marriage between you and Manuel. I wanted what was best for you.'

'No. You wanted what was best for you, and it backfired. Manuel wants only to be a priest.'

'He is not the only one who wants!' he said harshly, his eyes bleak. Then his face changed and he drew himself up to his full height. 'But come, our guests must be wondering where we are.'

There were so many guests Joanna doubted if anyone but Elena had missed them. Towards evening she found herself searching the crowded rooms for Manuel. Then she caught sight of Josefa carrying a tray of champagne.

'Have you seen Manuel?' she asked. 'I've been looking for him and can't find him in this crowd. The last time I saw him was at church this morning.'

A brief flash of pain seared Josefa's face, but she merely handed Joanna a glass and turned away. 'No, *señora*, I have not seen him.'

But she wouldn't be put off. 'You know something! He isn't here, is he?'

'Please, *señora*, do not ask.'

'But why? Why isn't he here? Has something happened to him? Come to think of it, he was acting strange this morning. And the way he said goodbye——'

Just then Rafael came across the *sala* to her. 'Is anything wrong, Josefa?'

She dipped her head. 'No, *señor*. I think it is time for all of you to sit down in the dining room.'

'I've been asking Josefa if she knew where Manuel is,' Joanna said with a frown. 'I haven't seen him all day.'

'He has taken Isabel back to her home in Madrid,' he said coldly, his face twisting. 'Under the circumstances, I did not wish her to be a party to this farce.'

Joanna choked back a gasp. 'But surely she could have waited until tomorrow? Manuel must have wanted to join in this celebration. After all, he engineered it.'

'Manuel cannot always have what he wants!'

The words as well as the coldness of his tone stung, but she raised her chin and put her hand on his outstretched arm. 'I guess there's nothing more to say, then. Shall we go in to dinner?'

She made a determined effort to see that Rafael's guests enjoyed themselves, but throughout the elaborate seven-course wedding feast she kept thinking of Manuel and how much he would have enjoyed it.

Josefa had outdone herself. There was everything from a variety of seafood, anchovies and eel to shrimp and lobster, and egg dishes of every kind. Salads and exotic vegetables were passed up and down the table, followed by cold meats, and finally the hot dishes of mussels in clam broth and flaming shish-kebab.

Joanna could imagine what Manuel would have made of that, with his sense of humour.

'You must forget my brother now,' said Rafael in a low voice.

Her sudden blush told him he had read her thoughts accurately, but she didn't say anything.

'This is our wedding day. It is an insult to me to let any other man occupy your thoughts.'

Her eyes flew up to his. 'Do you care?'

'Some of our guests are very perceptive.' He was leaning towards her, smiling as if whispering an endearment. 'Only a little while longer, then the charade will be over.'

But Joanna didn't think the evening would ever end. It was extremely late when the last guests said their farewells, and her face felt stiff from keeping a smile on it.

Elena Vegas was the last to leave, and to Joanna's relief, she ignored her completely. 'Will I see you in Madrid tomorrow, Rafe?' Her voice was a seductive whisper.

All at once Joanna saw red. Couldn't she have the decency to let her pretend to have a honeymoon? She couldn't hear what he answered. Her eyes squeezed shut and the blood roared in her ears. When she opened them again they were alone in the bright marble hall.

'I know you are tired, Joanna, but there is one more thing before you retire. Come.' Rafael flexed his shoulders wearily, the first sign of human weakness he showed all day. 'It will only take a moment.'

She followed him unsteadily up the stairway before stopping at one of the long windows.

'There.' He pointed, and she was surprised to see the dark sky alight with a brilliant explosion of colour. 'It is for us,' he said quietly. 'All day the villagers have been holding their own celebration, even though we were not expected to attend. Now it is finished. The fireworks mark the end of the celebration. Life for them will once again resume its own sedate pattern.'

Joanna stared at the sparkling sky and marvelled at the customs of this country. The poor people of the village had their own form of celebrating to show they were happy for their *duque* and they weren't the least bit slighted when he didn't take part in it. He had remained aloof with all his wealthy friends in his palace at the top of the hill, and somehow she was saddened at the unfairness of it. If she'd had a choice, she didn't doubt she would have had a much nicer time at the simpler celebration, getting the feel of the real Spain, than at the more elaborate one that seemed to her like an overdone cocktail party.

Rafael watched her for a long moment, reading her expression before turning away. 'They would not enjoy living as my equals, Joanna. They are simple people and will remain so. Goodnight, my—*duquesa*.'

She reached up and carefully lifted the *mantilla* and comb from her head. 'Thank you,' she said softly, her voice a mere thread of sound, 'for letting me use your mother's *mantilla*. It was good of you to loan it to me under the circumstances—I almost felt like a real bride in it.' Shaking, she pushed it into his hands, then quickly turned and fled to her room with the white lace dress flaring out behind her.

It wouldn't do for Rafael to see her cry. All day she had kept up the pretence. She wouldn't let him see just how shallow it was. Her heart was breaking. She loved him and sometimes she hated him, but she could never feel one ounce of pity for him.

He had given her his title, his wealth and a place in his home, but he wouldn't accept her meagre offering of love in return. She flung herself across her bed, uncaring that she was crushing the delicate lace gown that must have cost him the earth, and allowed herself the luxury of tears.

How could I do this? she thought miserably, and then she told herself to stop this self-pity. It wouldn't do any good. I knew what I was doing. I had a choice and I made it. What's done is done and I'll go on from here. She straightened and scrubbed away her tears, trying to regain control of her emotions, then walked over to pull the silk cord that would bring her maid to her.

She had unfastened as many of the little satin buttons as she could reach, but Brigida hadn't come yet. She unpinned her hair and brushed it until it shone, then pulled the cord again and waited. Still Brigida didn't come. Where was she?

Everything was quiet and still in the hallway when she looked out and all the lamps had been extinguished for the night. She sighed. All the servants were probably asleep, since it was after four o'clock in the morning. But what was she going to do? She twisted and struggled with both hands behind her, but there was no way to undo the buttons. If she pulled the dress any farther, the lace would rip. Taking a deep breath, she stepped down the hall and knocked softly at Rafael's door.

'What is it?' he answered at once in a low harsh voice.

'I'm sorry to bother you,' she said, pushing open the door, then stiffened in surprise.

He was standing at his window wearing only black slacks when he whirled around and saw her there. He crossed swiftly to his bed and picked up his shirt, flinging it across his shoulders, but she had already seen what he tried to hide.

Across the rippling muscles of his back and shoulders was a network of ugly white horn welts that criss-crossed their way drunkenly down his back. She glimpsed a peculiarly shaped thick patch for only a second before realising it was a hoofprint.

Unconsciously her hands clenched and something like pain snaked its way to her heart as she imagined the horrors he must have endured. A shudder passed through her and her widened eyes flew to his face, but he had seen the involuntary reaction and his face twisted into a derisive sneer, daring her to comment.

'What do you want?' he muttered savagely before fumbling with his shirt, trying to put it on.

'Please leave it off. I've already seen it.' Her voice wobbled as she struggled to maintain a calm look.

'I will not tolerate your pity!'

The words were like cold water splashed in her face, and they gave her the equilibrium she sought. 'I told you before, you haven't got my pity. All day long I've heard what a great bullfighter you were. I never thought you'd escaped with only the scar on your face.'

'I saw the revulsion you could not hide. Do not tell me you were not shocked.'

'It's not revulsion. Those scars are part of you. I've never known you any other way, so how can you say I'm revolted? I was surprised at your reaction, not shocked at your scars.' Her eyes blazed as she watched him put on his shirt and button it with stiff fingers. 'And as for pity, I'm surprised you're able to walk upright. I should think with all your self-pity you'd have to wallow!'

The angry fire of his eyes scorched her. '*Santo Dios!* I am tired of you always lashing out at me as if I were your whipping boy. I will no longer listen to your insults!' He moved towards her with the swiftness of a panther and his arms shot out to imprison her shoulders to give her a rough shaking, but the instant he touched her, all thought of angry retaliation fled. He drew her roughly against him in the powerful circle of his arms.

Instead of trying to pull away, she willingly curved herself against his lean muscular body, feeling his lips against her hair and delighting in what sounded like a groan coming from the very depths of his soul. Her mouth moved up to meet his in a searing kiss that left her weak and trembling. His lips were firm and warm as he held her to him. His shirt had been haphazardly buttoned and she pushed it open to run her hands over his chest, to tangle her fingers in the soft cloud of curling hair before resting on a thick patch of puckered skin over his heart where he had been gored.

'No!' he groaned harshly, pushing her away from him.

'Why are you afraid to let me get close to you?' she cried, stricken at the harsh glitter in his black eyes. 'Won't you believe I love you and would never hurt you?'

Rafael ran distracted fingers through his hair. 'I had to learn a painful lesson at the hands of a woman. I will not allow it to happen again.' He turned abruptly away.

'How can you let Elena hold such power over you? Surely your pride is stronger than that? She might have thought your scars hideous once, but it's obvious she's revised her opinion now. Doesn't that restore your confidence?' Joanna watched him helplessly, her eyes enormous with hurt, her heart beating in thick painful strokes at the grim set of his unrelenting jaw.

'I am not talking about Elena.' He rubbed the back of his neck and flexed his shoulders wearily.

'Then who?'

'I do not wish to speak of it.' His cold dark eyes flicked over her, effectively cutting off her retort. 'Why are you not in bed asleep? You must be tired?'

She blushed a bright red and twisted her hands together. 'I can't undo this dress. I rang for Brigida, but she must be asleep. None of the other servants answered either. There was no one else I could ask.'

Without a word he stepped behind her and began unbuttoning the satin buttons. Once he muttered: 'Be still! The buttons are small and my fingers are clumsy.' His voice was oddly thick and didn't sound at all like him.

She lifted the heavy length of her hair to keep it out of his way, trying not to tremble at the touch of his cool fingers on her back. His nearness was a powerful stimulant and she was overwhelmed with the desire to fling herself into his arms, but she knew she was only inviting another rejection.

He was nearly at the end of the long row when she turned, stung by his indifference and her own terrible feeling of inadequacy. Didn't she mean anything to him? Couldn't she at least arouse his desire if nothing else?

'Please, Rafael, I'm your wife now. Won't you relax

your guard and show some emotion? Won't you tell me what's making you so cold and callous? I have a right to know.'

'A right?' Grim hauteur twisted his face. 'You have no rights, Joanna. You are my *duquesa*, not my wife.'

'Please, I only want to help you.' The pleading in her eyes was suddenly replaced by a dawning comprehension and she became very still. It wasn't Elena at all! 'What did Matilda do that was so terrible?' she asked gently.

He closed his eyes as the pain stole over his face and ran a hand through his hair, ruffling it and making him look oddly vulnerable. 'Must you keep pecking away at me? Can you not leave things the way they are?' His accent thickened and she knew he was upset.

She stepped closer to him and put a hand on his arm, surprised when he didn't flinch away. 'It's not good to keep everything bottled up like a festering wound. Bring it out in the open. Take a good look at it and maybe it'll lose its power over you.'

'You do not know what you are saying.'

She stared hard at him, seeing the weariness in his face, the deeply etched lines of pain and the thick black hair liberally sprinkled with grey. She sighed heavily, her voice barely a whisper. 'I should have known better. With your pride, you couldn't let me help you.'

He said nothing, just stared at her, his eyes dark and unfathomable, his face expressionless as if carved from stone.

'Forgive me, Rafael. It's true, I haven't any rights.' She turned quickly, but he reached out and barred her way.

'Joanna.' His voice shook and then without another word, he pulled her into his arms, burying his face in her golden hair.

She pressed herself to his chest and hid the compassion in her eyes. For a long time she stayed like that, content just to be close to him, listening to the unsteady rhythm of his heart. She wanted to stay here, to love him, to help ease the pain that gnawed at his proud heart. 'Matilda didn't love you. If she had, she wouldn't have hurt you,' she said unsteadily.

Rafael spanned her back with his strong hands and set her a little way away from him within the circle of his arms, trying to pull himself together. When he finally spoke his voice was flat. 'I always knew Matilda did not love me. It was an arranged marriage, as was the custom. She wanted to become the Duquesa and that was enough for me. Her family was noble and wealthy, as was mine. I thought she had integrity, if nothing else. I thought she had some dignity and pride, that eventually she would return my affection.'

His fingers unconsciously bit into her shoulders, bruising them. 'She quickly became bored with being my wife and living in this village. And she did not want to be a mother. She said I had Manuel to care for and that was enough. I did not need sons of my own. We argued many times and, finally, one night she ran away with her lover.'

'What!' Joanna's breath caught harshly in her throat.

He let her go and ran a hand over his haggard face. 'Elena had a brother, Ramón, who was everything I was not: handsome, charming, irresponsible. He had no position to uphold. He could come and go as he pleased with no restrictions placed on him because of noble titles. He wanted only a "good time". He had much money and he was self-centred, thinking only of the shallow comfort his wealth could bring him. He was Matilda's ideal.

'She was leaving me when their car skidded on the road. Ramón died instantly, but Matilda had internal injuries that caused her to suffer much before she died several hours later. My friend Sergeant Rivera notified me and she was brought here so there would be no scandal. No one knows what happened that night aside from myself and Sergeant Rivera. Josefa has guessed some of it, but even she does not know everything.' He looked at her pale face. 'And now I have told you.'

In spite of herself Joanna felt a deep sympathy for him, but she crushed it, knowing his pride could never accept it. 'You can't change the past. You must put it behind you.'

'No, that I will not do. I was an utter fool, but no woman will ever make a fool of me again. I did not love Matilda, but I had some affection for her and I trusted her. She deceived me. I will never give you that chance.'

'But that's not fair! We could be happy together if only you didn't hide behind the memory of a woman who hurt you.' She stared at the harsh outline of his face with frustration.

'That is enough, Joanna. Do not speak to me this way.'

'Someone has to. How can you give up living because you've been hurt? Do you think you're the only one this ever happened to? I know you can't think that.'

'You do not know me at all.' He stood close to her, his anger seething. 'You are in Spain now, where wives do not deceive their husbands. Such a thing is not tolerated.'

'Oh, stop it! People are people no matter where they live. Why is it all right for Spanish husbands to have mistresses but Spanish wives aren't supposed to look at other men? Matilda probably knew about you and Elena. Don't you think that was a blow to her pride too?'

'You will say no more! You do not know what you are saying.'

'And you have no intention of enlightening me either, have you? You'd rather keep everything locked up inside you in that empty place where your heart used to be.' Joanna stared into the burning depths of his black eyes and shivered before gathering up the trailing skirts of her wedding gown. His dark brooding tallness intensified the dim space separating them. 'I love you, Rafael, even though neither of us wanted it this way. I'm glad you told me about your wife, but don't expect me to turn a blind eye to your association with Elena. You've got yourself an English wife now, whether you want me or not!'

She turned then and left him.

CHAPTER SEVEN

JOANNA didn't know what to expect the next morning, but she certainly didn't expect Rafael to be standing beside her bed watching her struggle up through the thinning mists of sleep. She brushed back the shining hair spilling across her pillow and drew her hand across her eyes, blinking against the strong sunlight flooding the room. Glancing about sleepily, she saw him and struggled up in surprise, dragging the sheet up to her chin.

He was wearing dark slacks and a white shirt with flowing sleeves gathered at the wrists. It suited him this morning, giving him a roguish, piratical appearance. His dark eyes held a strange intent look, but in a lightning instant, a shutter closed over them.

'*Buenos dias*, Joanna. I trust you slept well?' His voice was cool and detached. Last night might have been a figment of her imagination. He certainly didn't look as if any harsh words had passed between them or that they had parted in anger.

'I must have slept,' she said in confusion. 'I hadn't thought I'd sleep at all.'

'I am sorry to awaken you at this hour, but if we are to start our journey to Burgos, Brigida must pack your cases.'

His voice hardened. 'She omitted to do so yesterday.'

Joanna blushed a fiery red. 'Please don't blame her. I'm not used to having people do things for me. I told her I'd take care of it myself.'

'You are a *duquesa* now. It is the custom to have servants.'

She bent her head to hide her annoyance at this loss of the last of her independence. 'I'll—try—to remember,' she said in a tight voice.

'I should not think you would find it difficult to adjust to a life of luxury. If you were a wealthy woman trying to adjust to poverty then you might run into difficulty.'

She flung her bright head back, confused by the sneer in his voice. 'That's what Manuel intends to do now. Are you looking down on him for accepting the poverty of the priesthood?'

He stiffened and his eyes blazed with rage. 'I must ask you to refrain from speaking of Manuel again.'

'Refrain——?' She forgot she was clad only in an ivory satin nightgown and the sheet fell away as she knelt on the bed facing him. 'And what about when he comes back from Madrid? Won't I be allowed to talk to him?'

'He will not be coming back.'

She caught her breath. 'Why?'

He faced her squarely, his hands clenched by his sides. 'We will not speak of it.'

'Because he put one over on you?' She closed her eyes and the room spun. 'Oh, Rafael,' she slid from the bed and stood trembling in front of him, 'don't be angry with him for that. Don't you see? He knew how much I loved you. He knew I could never marry him. This was the only thing he could do.'

'Enough!'

'No, I won't be silenced. You can't send him away.'

'He has done it himself.'

'Because he loved you—as much as I do.'

His eyes narrowed and swept over her pale face for a long disturbing moment. 'If he loved me he could have chosen to give up the priesthood and take his rightful place in this family. Now he has no choice at all.'

'What do you mean?'

'Just what I have said. He has been banished, stripped of his name and any claim to my possessions. And he will never be a priest.'

Joanna stood stricken, her head moving from side to side as if a hidden string was making her continue the negative movement against her will. 'No, you can't do this! You mustn't. He's your brother, Rafael! I'm nothing to you, but he's your own flesh and blood. You can't turn him out like this—because of me!'

'It is done.'

She lost all her colour and swayed unsteadily, remembering Manuel as she had last seen him. He had been at the church and he had gripped her hands and said goodbye to her with a fierceness that surprised her at the time. But now it was all so clear. It really was goodbye!

'You ordered him to leave yesterday, didn't you? That's why he wasn't at the reception. He didn't take your aunt to Madrid, did he?'

'He did not. Isabel refused to stay and left directly from the church. I do not know where Manuel has gone and you are forbidden to try to contact him in any way. It will be as if he is dead.'

'But he's your brother!'

'I no longer have a brother.'

'He only wanted you to be happy. He thought *I* could make you happy.' Huge tears sprang to her eyes. 'Don't you see? He was desperate.'

'Oh yes, he told me you did not love each other. He

could not marry you knowing you loved me. And you do love me, do you not?' Rafael's face darkened and he stepped closer to her. 'Tell me now how much you love me.'

'You're the most despicable man I know!' Her throat felt tight and she found breathing difficult. 'Have you always treated those who dare to love you with such cruelty? Or is it just Manuel and me?'

'You do not love me, Joanna. At first you were intrigued by the fact that I was a *matador*. You thought it a romantic profession. The second day you were here, you were grateful to me because I comforted you when your friends died in the plane crash. You were grateful until you learned why I took you to Malaga. And then later you pitied me because you thought Elena was repulsed by my scars. You were so transparent! I did not care then if you believed this because it suited my purpose, but I will tell you the truth now, so you will know just how cruel I can be. Elena did not leave me when I nearly died from my wounds. She would have stayed, but I had told her earlier that day, before the fight, that I did not love her and would never marry her. I used her, Joanna, to get my revenge on her brother.'

She put a shaking hand to her mouth, her voice barely forcing its way past the huge dry lump in her throat. 'Have you no conscience?'

'No! Now you are no longer intrigued and no longer grateful, but you still pity me and I will not tolerate it.'

'Pity!' Her voice burst from her. 'You couldn't be more wrong. There's a difference between pity and compassion, just as there's a difference between pride and conceit. I thought you had a great deal of pride, but I see now how wrong I was. You're not proud. You're a conceited, arrogant man and I'm sorry I ever had the misfortune of running into Manuel and meeting you!'

'It was a misfortune in every way. But you have married me and you shall stay married to me. You are my *duquesa* by your own choice and now you have the responsibility that goes with the wealth and the title.' He thrust his head back. 'So now we know everything there is to know about each other.'

'You haven't even begun to know me,' she exclaimed savagely. 'I don't think you ever will!' She turned away from his sneering face.

Rafael nodded coldly. 'I shall keep that thought in mind. I have made plane reservations for two o'clock this afternoon. Will that give you enough time to be ready?'

'If I'm allowed any choice in the matter, I'd rather not go to Burgos.'

'Have you changed your mind? I thought it was a place you dreamed of seeing.'

Joanna lifted her chin higher. 'This is one dream I don't want to lose, Rafael. All the others have been shattered. At least let me keep this one.'

El Cid had been born there. He lived and loved there and now somewhere in that city, in a huge cathedral, an ornate tomb held his remains and those of his wife. Joanna didn't want to walk over that holy ground with an unfeeling stranger by her side. She wanted to share it with the man who loved her, who could feel what she felt.

'Very well,' he said coldly. 'We shall stay here pretending to be lovers in seclusion. It is much better this way. The pretence of a honeymoon would have been more than I could stand.' With haughty dignity, he turned on his heel and left her.

This is the way it'll be from now on, Joanna thought, watching him go. We'll be polite strangers in front of the servants and bitter antagonists whenever we're alone.

And to think I actually thought my love would change him. I was going to make him love me! She laughed bitterly. What a fool, what a blind romantic fool I am!

Their relationship underwent a drastic change from that day on, until one particularly hot sultry afternoon two months later when Joanna chanced to walk to the village.

She had been a virtual prisoner in the ducal palace. Each morning Rafael had coldly taken over the task of moulding her into a proper *duquesa*. He began by teaching her his language, pointing out different objects and giving her the Spanish word for each one. She would stiffly repeat it over and over, trying to match his accent.

But those few hours each morning were unbearable. The constraint between them was a stumbling block to her progress. Sometimes he would correct her pronunciation with biting sarcasm. Other times he would completely unnerve her with his cold, silent, penetrating stare.

After these morning sessions he would disappear until they met again for dinner at ten o'clock in the evening. Usually they sat alone, in silence, at the long table and ate sparingly because neither of them had an appetite. Rafael acted as if he could hardly bear her company. Whenever she felt his booding gaze on her, she would look up quickly, but he would avert his eyes with a heavy scowl.

The days were long and time dragged by with agonising slowness, but the nights were never-ending. Lying awake, Joanna would listen to her husband moving about his room and wonder what he was thinking. They rarely spoke to each other and she became thinner, grimmer and more silent.

There was nothing for her to do in the palace. Soft-footed servants anticipated her every wish and were quick to do things for her. She didn't have the heart to tell them she would rather do them herself.

On this particular afternoon, she came up the grassy

track from the beach where she had been sunbathing. Her tan was becoming a deep gold, but it made no difference to her; Rafael never noticed. Her steps were slow across the courtyard and suddenly her mind balked at the thought of going back into her elegant prison. Without a word to anyone, she straightened the skirt of her white sundress over her bathing suit and turned her steps towards the village. She had no destination in mind; she just had to get away for a few hours.

The afternoon sun was broiling and she found breathing difficult because she wasn't used to walking such a distance in such heat. By the time she reached the old well in the centre of the village, she felt dizzy and dangerously close to tears. Several people saw her progress and, recognising her, shyly murmured words of greeting.

Joanna tried to respond, but everything spun sickeningly before a dull roar sounded in her ears and then a black void opened up to swallow her.

When she opened her eyes again, she found herself on a narrow bed in a small whitewashed room that was exceptionally clean and blessedly cool. Just as she sat up, the door opened and a tall thin young man dressed in wrinkled white clothes came in with a worried frown on his dark face.

She blinked in disbelief. 'You!' She closed her eyes, then opened them again as if she expected him to have disappeared. 'Is it really you, Manuel?'

'*Si.*' He gave her a wide welcoming grin and shyly sat on a small chair close to the bed.

She put a hand on his arm. 'Really? I'm not just dreaming?'

'I am here, Joanna.' He took both her hands in his. 'Are you all right?'

'Just a little dizzy. What happened? Where am I? How

did you get here? Oh, Manuel, I can't believe it's you after all this time!'

He laughed at her rapid-fire questions. 'I think you fainted. Our summer afternoons are not meant for walking long distances, especially without a hat.' He grinned, remembering the awful monstrosity he had bought for her so long ago. 'Some of the children saw you by the well and thought you were ill. They came for me at once.'

'You live in the village? All this time you've been here?'

'*Si*. I live with Father Esteban. I am helping in his clinic for the sick.'

'But he never said anything. Every time I asked, he said he had no word from you. Every day Josefa and I questioned the servants, but no one could tell us anything.'

Manuel's face darkened but he was silent.

'You must have known we'd be worried about you? Couldn't you have sent word to us?' She angrily snatched her hands away from his.

'You must know I was forbidden to contact you in any way. If anyone asked if I was here, he was told I was not. And Father Esteban was not allowed to say anything either.'

Joanna turned her face away and groaned. 'Why?'

'I will try to explain, but first—my brother? He is happy?'

She swallowed jerkily. 'He's as happy as he'll allow himself to be.'

His dark eyes clouded with sadness. 'I see.' He stood then and rubbed the back of his neck, and suddenly she saw that he looked thinner and older than before. She saw too that his shirt was rough white cotton instead of fine silk and his white slacks were shapeless and baggy and hung on his slender hips.

'Nothing is ever the way we plan it to be, is it?' he said sadly. 'I wanted only happiness for my brother. I thought you could give him this. And in his happiness I thought I could find my own. I gambled and lost. He insisted I follow his plan for my life, but I see now that, as much as he loved me, he could not allow me to better him, so he did the only thing he could do. He refused to give me permission to enter the seminary. He disowned me. He told me I was to leave and never contact him or anyone in his household again.'

'And that's it? You're not doing anything about it?'

'There is nothing I can do.'

'I don't believe it!' she said bitterly, coming to stand shakily behind him. 'There has to be someone who can reach him, someone who can make him see how wrong he is.'

'You are his wife. You must know his pride is no small thing. It is what makes him the great *duque* he is.'

She scowled at him. 'But I thought you wanted to be a priest? That you'd do *anything* to pursue this vocation? Look at the way you manipulated me! Yet here you are, ready to play dead just because Rafael has too much pride to admit you bettered him. I'm surprised at you, Manuel!'

'Ah, Joanna,' he grinned, 'how can Rafael not be happy with you for his wife?'

She clenched her fists frustratedly. 'I won't give up, even if you have.'

His smile was affectionate. 'Come, if you are feeling better we will find Father Esteban and have a cool drink. Would you like to see the good work we are doing here in the clinic?'

'I'd like that—but don't think I can sit back and let things stay the way they are between you and your brother. It's gone on long enough, don't you think?'

'If anyone can do anything,' he grinned, 'you are the one to do it.'

By the time Joanna left the village there was a lightness to her step and a sparkle in her eyes that had been missing for a long time. She and Josefa sat together in the bright sunny kitchen pouring out their mutual relief at having found Manuel.

'Yes, he's fine,' Joanna assured her. 'You should see what he's doing. And how the people love him! He's so good with the little children.'

Josefa wiped away her happy tears. 'I am so glad you have spoken to him, *señora*. I have been so worried.'

'Now that we know where he is, I intend to see him often.'

'But how will you do this?'

'Every afternoon I sit around here with nothing to do. I'm going crazy with nothing to keep me busy. Father Esteban said if I really wanted to help, there was enough work to keep ten people busy. And I'll be practising my Spanish too. So you see, it's not such a bad idea.'

'But when Don Rafael finds out he will be angry. You are the Duquesa. You should not do this.'

'But he won't find out. That's where you come in. You've got to cover for me, Josefa. Rafael's never around in the afternoons. But if he should happen to look for me, you can tell him I'm resting or I'm down by the sea or something.'

'I do not know. It is good that you have found Manuel, but you have a title now. You should not work among the *peones*. They will not respect you.'

'They'll see I'm human just like they are.'

'But Don Rafael will find out. He will be furious!'

'Oh, come on. Did Manuel have this hard a time getting you to go along with his schemes? I was gone today and the great Duque didn't miss me. Even you didn't know I was gone. It'll work, I know it will.'

And this arrangement did work—for nearly a week.

Late one evening Joanna scrambled into the courtyard hot and dishevelled. Josefa had been watching for her and practically ran past the gurgling fountain to her.

'*Señora!* You are so late. What happened?' She twisted her hands nervously and kept glancing back over her shoulder. 'Don Rafael is acting like a wounded bull. I knew this would happen. He missed you early and has been searching everywhere for you.'

'Not today of all days!' Joanna groaned, running a distracted hand through her windblown hair. 'The baby I've been taking care of has been running a high temperature and refuses to let anyone near him but me.'

'The one who was abandoned?'

She nodded, breathing a worried sigh. 'He's become attached to me.'

'But, *señora*, this is terrible! Is for certain Don Rafael will find out where you have been.'

'What did you tell him?'

'I told him I did not know where you were. I suggested he look on the beach.'

'And did he?'

Josefa nodded. 'He came back furious.'

'Oh no!' Joanna bit her lip. 'And I told Manuel I'd come back this evening as soon as I could get away.'

'But you cannot do this! Don Rafael will want to know where you are going.'

'I'll just have to slip away after dinner—but I'll need your help. Will you telephone Father Esteban when Rafael is finished eating? He usually goes to his study then and won't notice if I'm gone. Father Esteban told me he'd send a car for me.'

'You know I would do anything for you, *señora*, but this is madness!' protested Josefa.

'I have to go.' Joanna chewed her lip nervously. 'That

baby means so much to me. He was just left on the door-step and they still haven't found his parents. I love him as if he were my own!'

'Oh, you are asking for big trouble.'

'I'll be in bigger trouble if I don't change and get into dinner!' Joanna forced a smile to her face and quickly went into the house.

By the time she had showered and changed, she was a bundle of nerves. She and Brigida were struggling with the zipper of a long midnight blue dress when Rafael came into the room with a thunderous scowl on his face. He coldly dismissed Brigida and stood staring at Joanna with his arms folded in front of his powerful chest.

'Where have you been, Joanna?'

With her arms behind her back she gripped her dress together and stared at him with enormous eyes. He looked so unapproachable in his black dinner jacket and matching slacks with their knife-edge crease, his stark white shirt making him look darker and more alien.

'Answer me!' he ground out savagely.

'I—I've been in the village.'

'Why?'

She swallowed convulsively. 'I was—visiting—Father Esteban and—and the time just got away from me.'

'You expect me to believe that?'

'It's the truth.' Stretched a little but nevertheless the truth, she thought.

His mouth thinned. 'And how is the good Father? Still saving souls?' he jeered.

'He's fine, and he sends you his regards.'

'No!' he thundered. 'How can you lie to me? It was not Father Esteban who brought you home.' With dangerously glittering eyes he stepped closer to her. 'I saw you from my window when you returned. Why did you not have the car bring you to the door? Were you afraid I would see you with another man? You were acting so very guilty.'

Joanna swallowed and forced herself to laugh lightly. 'Guilty? Really, Rafael, you've developed a wild imagination! That was Pedro Morales, a friend of Father Esteban, who brought me home. He was there the same time that I was and offered to take me home. Would you rather I refused and have him think his *duquesa* was a snob?' She licked her suddenly dry lips. 'It was a bumpy ride and rather than hurt his feelings, I told him I'd walk the rest of the way since I was so close to home.'

Rafael blinked uncertainly and she knew he didn't expect her to give him such a calm rational answer. 'Are you telling the truth?'

'You know I'd never lie to you.' She stood up straighter and held her chin high.

'No,' he conceded after a moment, 'that is one thing you have never done.' Without warning he put his hands on her shoulders and turned her around. 'May I help you with this zipper? All good husbands do this for their wives, do they not?'

His fingers were cool against her skin and she tried to stand still. This was the last thing she had expected from him. He had been so cold for so long and now he was acting like a loving husband. It completely threw her.

As the zipper slid up easily, she tried to control her shivers. His breath was warm and for a shuddering instant she felt his lips brush the side of her neck. He muttered something in rapid Spanish before turning away. She gulped and felt a rush of heat spread up her face.

With a violent gesture he strode to the door and held it open. 'Josefa is waiting to serve dinner,' he said coldly.

I'll never understand him, she thought. Was he doing this deliberately? After treating her with icy disdain for so long, the touch of his lips made her weak with longing, but just as suddenly he became cold again.

She jabbed her fork at a piece of chicken and pushed it around her plate, staring into space.

'What has happened to your appetite, Joanna?' Rafael snapped harshly. 'This past week I thought you were finally beginning to enjoy our Spanish meals, but tonight you are merely pushing the food around.'

Guilty colour rushed to her face. 'I—I'm just not hungry.'

'What happened today?'

'Nothing!' she said a little too quickly before controlling herself. 'What could possibly have happened?'

'You tell me.' His voice was icy. 'What made you decide to visit Father Esteban today?'

Joanna dipped her head, pretending to be absorbed in her plate. 'Oh, I just thought he'd enjoy the company. He did tell us on our wedding day that we were welcome any time.'

Rafael's face darkened into a forbidding scowl and his eyes roamed over her flushed face. 'And this innocent visit to a priest has suddenly made you change? You look different this evening. You are no longer wan and pale. Even your eyes have fire in them.'

She squirmed on her chair. Why wasn't she able to hide her feelings the way he did? 'It couldn't be because you've started acting like a husband, could it? Usually you try to pretend I'm not here.'

'Is that what you want, Joanna?' he said too quietly. 'Do you want me to be your husband?'

She jerked her head up and stared straight into his burning black scowl, then her eyes flickered involuntarily to his scar. There was nothing she wanted more. But a husband without love? She shivered.

He deliberately raised his wine glass and drank down its contents all the while holding her gaze. 'Do not worry, you do not have to be afraid of me. I would not force myself on you. You must forgive my—momentary lapse earlier. Let us just say I was worried when I could not find you this afternoon and I was—carried away—with relief when I found in all innocence you had been visiting with the good Father.' His mouth thinned to a grim line and his expression was full of mockery.

Joanna stood up desperately and looked at him. 'Please excuse me, Rafael. I have a headache and I'm a little tired. If you don't mind, I'll just go to bed.'

'But of course,' he said with a wide understanding smile before tossing down another glass of wine. 'Shall I send Josefa to you? Perhaps she can give you something for your—headache.' He was all innocence, and she was suddenly afraid.

'Yes,' she whispered, 'please ask Josefa to come.'

She walked quickly from the room and ran up the stairs as if someone was chasing her. Only when she closed the door to her room did she feel safe. It was absurd—Rafael couldn't know she had found Manuel and was helping him in the clinic.

Yet the feeling that he was aware of all her movements persisted long after the house became silent. She waited an interminable length of time before judging it safe to leave, and by the time she was again at the clinic, her heart was thumping uncomfortably and the headache she had feigned had become a reality.

The evening was cool and all the windows were opened wide, but even though she had changed into a simple navy blue skirt and white cotton blouse, nervous perspiration made the clothes stick to her.

'Did my brother suspect something this evening?' Manuel asked as he stood beside her, watching the baby drift into an uneasy slumber.

'I'm afraid so,' she answered unsteadily. Her fingers

gently caressed the tiny forehead and she sighed. 'It's awfully late and I've been gone a long time. I'd better go.' Straightening reluctantly, she gave Manuel a wan smile. 'Don't hesitate to ring if you need me.'

'I cannot help thinking what Rafael will do when he finds out you come here. If I ring you, he will know.'

Joanna stiffened her shoulders, mentally picturing Rafael's face when he found out. 'I'm afraid this baby means so much to me I'll risk his anger.'

'You will make a good mother,' he said gently. The tired lines of his handsome dark face changed to an irrepressible grin. 'I knew that from the beginning.'

She shook her head wryly and gripped his shoulder with affectionate but nervous fingers before she tiptoed out.

In hardly any time at all her heart began to thump with maddening loudness as she once again crossed the shadowy courtyard on silent feet. The heavy front door swung open on noiseless hinges and she quickly skirted the dim shimmering puddles of moonlight on the marble floor in the hall. But before she reached the stairs, the darkness was replaced by the shattering brilliance of the huge crystal chandelier.

Rafael stood grimly with his hand on the light switch just outside his study door.

CHAPTER EIGHT

'WHERE have you been?' he asked in a deadly quiet voice.

Joanna couldn't say anything. Her heart was frozen in her throat. His unwavering stillness unnerved her more than ever before. She stared at him in terrified fascination and for the first time since they had been married she saw him without his façade of cold indifference. To her astonishment, pain stood out starkly in his eyes.

'I am waiting for an explanation.' He didn't move from his position by the door, but it was as if miles of frozen wasteland separated them. Across the width of the hall she could feel his barely restrained anger.

Her stricken eyes were enormous, but she remained mute.

'I have a right to know where my wife sneaks off to in the middle of the night. Did you really think I would not know?' His handsome face twisted into a sneer and his lips curled in distaste. 'You forget, I have been through this before. I know all the signs. For weeks now you have been unsettled, restless, bored. It was only natural for you to seek a diversion. And you found it, did you not? You have met someone. I know this because you could not disguise the fact that your life has suddenly changed this week. How like Matilda you are! I want an answer. Was he worth it?'

When he compared her to Matilda, her control snapped. Thinking only of the baby, Rodrigo, she faced him squarely, her chin thrust forward, her bright blue eyes blazing with angry fire. 'I won't lie to you,' she said clearly. 'He's worth everything I've had to go through this week.'

'You dare to say this to me?' he gritted in disbelief, staring at her for a long screaming moment before letting out his breath raggedly. 'At least you are not a liar like Matilda.' He laughed cruelly and turned away with a look of loathing. 'I want to meet him,' he said savagely as if having come to a sudden decision. His hands clenched and a muscle twitched in the side of his cheek. 'There will be no more sneaking behind my back. Divorce is frowned upon in my country, but it is not impossible. You shall have it, so you may go to him freely. But first, I want to meet this man. I want him to walk through that door so I can meet him face to face and hear from his own lips what he can give you that I have not, why he has had the audacity to take you away from me!' The muscles in his neck were standing out tautly as he turned to stare at her with unconcealed fury.

'He can't!' Joanna whispered, trying not to cower from his murderous look.

'I will not let you go until he walks through that door.'

'He can't walk,' she said stupidly.

'*Santo Dios!*' The words exploded from his throat. 'I might have known. Is your pity boundless? First you marry a scarred man whose very sight offends you, then you take up with a cripple!' He stood in front of her stunned and dazed. 'You cannot go until I meet him. And I shall meet him—now!'

'But it's two o'clock in the morning!'

Rafael folded his arms, staring at her, refusing to back down.

How could he think such terrible things? Had he absolutely no trust? With angry determination, she pushed past him to the telephone on his desk in his study. 'Very well, it shall be now.' She dialled and in a matter of minutes reached her connection. 'Manuel? Is Rodrigo awake? Will you please bring him here? Your brother wants to meet him.' There was silence for a moment, then she said: 'Yes, you heard me right. I realise the time, but since he's awake anyway, Rafael wants to meet him.'

She hung up the receiver and turned to stare at her husband with a face that was deathly pale. His harsh features were cold and fierce and unyielding.

'So, you have found my brother and he is a party to this treachery!'

'Oh, don't,' she pleaded. 'Don't say any more. You'll only say things you wish you hadn't.'

'I gave you everything, Joanna. Everything! And this is how you repay me.' He was full of wounded pride.

Her voice shook with hurt and outrage. 'You've given me everything but what I need. You've lavished your money on me and tried to teach me things, but you've never loved me! I told you your money means nothing to me. It's you I want and only you—to love me!'

'I do not believe I am hearing this. You speak of love, yet you have shown me you are like every other woman. You are not worthy of trust and love.' His face was pale, his voice hoarse. 'That very first night I thought you were different. You stood here in this room, so frightened yet so full of courage. You had nowhere to go, yet you dared to defy me, refusing my offer of help when I asked what it would take to make you change. I thought then you were different from other women.' He laughed harshly and the sound was mournful. 'But you have proved you are not different. You took everything from me, and now you have taken another man!'

Her face was white and her lips had a bluish tinge to them. 'I am different, Rafael. You judge all women by Elena's and Matilda's standards, but you're wrong. How do you think I feel, taking so much from you and not being able to give anything in return? I came to you with nothing, not even decent clothes on my back, yet when I offered you the only thing I have—my love—you refused me.'

'It was not love you offered. So many times I have seen the pity stark in your eyes.'

'Oh, you won't see it, will you? You're so busy protecting yourself against love you don't recognise it when it stares you in the face. I've never pitied you, but I've loved you so much for so long that I ache with the pain of it!' She felt the blood rush to her face in the sudden explosive silence.

Rafael's breathing was laboured. 'If you loved me so much, how could you turn to another man?'

'He's not——' But Joanna never finished the sentence, because just then the loud wail of an infant split the air.

Rafael's face, completely unguarded, was a study in astonishment. 'What is this?'

Manuel stood in the doorway of the study with the squealing Rodrigo held tightly in his arms, a look of uncertainty on his tired face. Brief seconds passed as the two men looked wordlessly at each other. Without taking his eyes away from Rafael, Manuel came farther into the room and stood before him, gripping the baby awkwardly.

Rafael's eyes flickered over him contemptuously and glittered with a dangerous brightness when they rested on the wildly flailing arms and legs in the pale blue blanket. 'What is the meaning of this?' he sneered angrily.

Manuel stood straight, not flinching under the stinging lash of Rafael's anger. 'Joanna asked me to bring Rodrigo.' He blinked uncertainly before dropping his eyes. 'Perhaps I misunderstood.'

'No, you didn't, Manuel.' Joanna took the baby in her arms. Immediately his sobs ceased and she held him close, looking up at Rafael. She found a certain satisfaction in having thrown him completely. 'This child is the reason I left tonight. He's been ill and I've been looking after him. All week, in the afternoons, I'd go to the village to help Father Esteban—and Manuel—in the clinic. Rodrigo's a difficult patient. He formed an attachment to me and sometimes he wakes late at night and refuses to go back to sleep until I come to him. I told Manuel to send for me any time he needed me. You and I see so little of each other, I never thought you'd notice if I was gone.' She stared at him bitterly before his eyes dropped.

He turned then and she saw the lines of strain around

his mouth, and suddenly he looked tired, more tired than she had ever seen him. He looked from Manuel to Joanna and then to the tiny baby. 'You have my apologies, all of you,' he said through clenched teeth. 'I have been an arrogant fool, concerned only with family pride and a ridiculous sense of honour that has long been outdated. It is no excuse for my behaviour to you.' His eyes locked with Manuel's for a long moment. 'As difficult as it is, you have my permission to enter the priesthood if you still wish it. I only hope your dreams will not be shattered. I have tried to protect you, but I see now I was wrong. You cannot help going your own way, just as I could not help going mine. You are welcome in your home at any time. I was wrong to banish you—it has not been the same since you left. Please—forgive me!'

There was silence. Both Joanna and Manuel knew what such an apology cost his pride. Then Manuel gave an exclamation of sheer joy.

'Rafael!' He threw his arms around his brother, amazed at the suggestion of moisture gathering in those dark eyes so like his own. After a moment he cleared his throat a little selfconsciously and stepped towards Joanna.

Rodrigo had started to cry again and she was trying without much success to soothe him. The tears were enormous in his jewel-black eyes. His nose was running and his plump little fist was jammed in his mouth.

'What is wrong with him?' Rafael asked in a hoarse voice.

'We're not sure. He's running a temperature and nothing pacifies him for long,' she said quietly.

'How old is he?' he asked, his eyes narrowing.

'Father Esteban estimates his age at six months,' Manuel said with a frown. 'He was left on the doorstep early in the week.'

Joanna shifted the baby in her arms and avoided looking at Rafael.

He studied her for a long tense moment, then crossed the room to a low cabinet at the side. He came back carrying a bottle of brandy and uncorked it, dipping his finger in the straw-coloured liquid. Without looking at Joanna, he crooned to the baby and began rubbing his gums with his brandy-coated finger.

Her eyes widened in surprise when Rodrigo immediately stopped crying and allowed Rafael to care for him.

'There you are, little one,' he said gently. 'That should help your teething pains.'

Joanna looked helplessly at Manuel. He stared back with equal consternation.

'But how did you know?' she gasped.

'Manuel was his age once, and it was not so long ago that I would forget. My father did this for him—just as yours did for you, no doubt. Here, Manuel, take the bottle and the child back to Father Esteban. I am sure he is concerned about him.' His eyes were dispassionate as he watched her give the baby back.

Manuel settled him contentedly in the crook of his arm and now that his gums were numbed, he drifted off to sleep instantly.

'I will let you know how he is in the morning, Joanna.' Manuel turned to his brother. 'It is all right if I telephone?'

'Of course.' His voice softened. 'Joanna will wish to know if he spent a restful night.' Then he spoke louder with an astuteness that surprised no one: 'And if Josefa is listening in the hall, she will wish to know too.'

Manuel nodded to both of them, then left the study with a sheepish grin.

The sound of a car died away in the distance and Josefa noisily made her way to her own room, then there was only silence in the study.

Rafael turned away and Joanna stood staring at his broad back. She saw his shoulders sag in defeat and his head dip forward. It tore at her heart to see such a proud man humbled. The silence continued, stretching endlessly.

Just when she thought he would never speak, his voice came out in a curious rustling whisper: 'I have been such a fool.'

'No, not a fool, Rafael. Just human like everybody else.'

He dragged a distracted hand through his hair and rubbed the back of his neck. 'Manuel has forgiven me. I did not think he would do this.'

'Manuel loves you. He told me earlier this week that you did what you had to do because you love him. He never doubted that for one minute.' Joanna bent her head and stared at the floor. 'I'm the only one who doubted you. Even Josefa told me I should try to understand, but I insisted you were an egotistical, self-opinionated, insufferable man who was too used to having his own way.'

A bitter smile crossed his face and he turned to her. 'I am all these things.'

She forced herself to meet his eyes. 'I know.'

His expression of defeat didn't change. 'If you want your freedom, I will not force you to stay. I am old and set in my ways. You are so young—seeing you with that child in your arms made me realise just how young you are. You should have many children of your own. I have no right to ask you to stay with me.'

Joanna turned away quickly, hiding the pain that seared through her. 'Rafael——' Her voice broke.

'No!' he interrupted harshly. In two strides he stood before her, arrogant power all about him. 'There was a time when I could have let you go.' With a groan of self-loathing, he hauled her into his arms and crushed her to his shuddering length. 'Forgive me. You will hate me for this, but I cannot let you walk out of my life. You are the only good thing that has ever happened to me.' His breath was harsh in his throat and his fingers tangled convulsively in her golden hair. 'I love you too much to let you go.' And then he was kissing her over and over, hungrily, urgently, until she had no doubts.

'I thought I'd never hear you say it,' she moaned, clinging shamelessly to him.

'I have been such a fool,' he muttered thickly, his lips roaming over every inch of her face and neck.

Her heart pounded madly. 'Yes, you have been.'

'I am a proud man, Joanna. You are not making this easy.'

'Easy? Do you know what you've put me through all this time? Every time I offered you my love, you threw it back at me.' She trembled in his arms.

'Forgive me!' He held her close against him, his hands fiercely gripping her back to still her shudders. 'I know you were forced into this marriage against your will. You have tried to make the best of it and I admire your courage. But love? Whenever you are close to me, I feel you shudder with revulsion. I know my scars sicken you, no matter how much you try to deny it.'

She stood absolutely still and stared at him with rounded eyes. 'What are you talking about?'

His hands roamed over her back where her blouse had pulled away from the waistband of her skirt, lingering on her heated skin, feeling her shudders. 'You see? Even now your flesh is revolted by my touch.'

'Oh, you stupid, stupid man! I don't know much about loving and wanting and needing. I thought I loved you, but you kept telling me I didn't, and you had me so confused that I didn't know any more if it really was love. All I know is the way I feel when I'm near you. I tingle and I can't seem to breathe right, and all I want is to feel your arms around me and press myself closer to you. I'm embarrassed by these feelings and I can't seem to control them. That's when I start to shake.'

Rafael looked at her in amazement. 'Do you mean that? You really do not know how to love a man?'

Joanna buried her flaming face in his chest. 'I thought you would teach me, my mentor. I have so much to learn. I want so much to know what pleases you.'

'Your mentor! How those words haunt me. I feel so much older than you, but I have never wanted to be your mentor. At the time it was the only way I could think to keep you here without frightening you. I could not bear to have you leave my house once I met you. I told you I wanted you for Manuel, I even convinced myself you were in love with him. You are young, you both have your whole lives ahead of you. But every time I looked at you I could not deny I want you for myself.'

'You do?' she breathed.

'You are all I have ever wanted. But I have led such a sordid life. I know I am not a good man. When I told you about Elena, you said you despised me. You made me even more ashamed of myself.' He released her and turned away, full of self-loathing.

'I'm sorry I said that.' Her eyes lingered on his tortured profile. 'But as much as I disliked Elena and as jealous as I am of her relationship with you, I thought it was a terrible thing for you to do. I was shocked at your deliberate cruelty.'

Rafael raked a distracted hand through his hair and she saw again how human he was. His eyes were haunted and he bowed his head. 'Do you not think I am filled with shame for what I did? Every time I looked at her I was reminded of how low I had sunk, of what a foul thing I had become. And there was no way I could make it right. Being with you only showed more clearly how sordid my life is.'

She put a hand on his arm. 'It's in the past. Let it stay there.'

'I thought I ruined Elena's happiness with my petty plan for revenge. I had no right to do that. She was not to blame for her brother's sins.'

'If she loves you enough, she'll forgive you.'

His face darkened and his eyes changed to a bitter and brooding blackness. 'No, she does not love me—she never did. I saw her this morning before she left for California with some film-maker she met. I crushed my pride and told her what I had done and begged her forgiveness, even as I have begged for yours this night.' His mouth twisted. 'She is a very shallow woman, Joanna. I never realised it before. When I tried to explain about Matilda and Ramón, she laughed at me.'

'Laughed?' Joanna was all sympathy.

'She knew all about it. All this time I thought I was saving my family honour! In my blind arrogance I was assured there was no scandal, that no one knew of the events of the fatal road accident. Yet all this time Elena and her parents knew. It seems Ramón had told them of his plans to take Matilda away from me. All this time she knew I was only using her. I did not know she was doing the same to me. She blamed Matilda for her brother's death. I did not touch her heart as I thought I did,' he finished with a rueful smile.

'My heart's the only one you've ever touched,' she said, her voice unsteady.

His arms slid around her waist, gathering her to him almost as if he could not help himself. He could feel her rapid heartbeat with intense satisfaction. 'Yes, my wife, and how it thunders with love!'

'You do believe that, don't you? It was never pity?'

'I want so much to believe you. I never should have doubted. But for you, Joanna, I would have spent the rest of my life brooding about how I thought I had hurt Elena and not knowing how to right the wrong.'

She touched her hand to the scar cleaving its path across his face, and for the first time since she met him, he didn't flinch.

'I have kept this scar to punish myself for hurting her. My mind was on her that afternoon, my last in the ring. Rather than concentrating on the bull, I kept thinking how shamelessly I had used her. My conscience had begun to bother me and that morning I told her I did not want to see her again. She demanded much money as recompense and I gave it to her. I thought I could buy an easy conscience. But then—this.' His fingers curled around her slender hand and held it against his cheek. 'Would you have me see a plastic surgeon?' His eyes burned with a glowing fire. 'It can be removed.'

'That scar is part of you, my love. I always thought it gave you an added distinction. But if it only brings back bitter memories, by all means have it removed.'

'I do not have to see it. Sometimes I forget it is there and must force myself to remember. But you will have to look at it for the rest of your life.' And then another thought struck him and he crushed her to him. 'What if our children think their father is hideous?'

Joanna laughed and blushed rosily, tracing her fingers across his face. 'They'll love you too much to think that. Rodrigo didn't notice it—in fact, I think he was quite taken with you. He's been so miserable for the past few days and five minutes after you saw him, you had him all figured out and comfortable again. You'll be such a good father.'

'I do not think so. Look at what I did to Manuel. I was arrogant and cruel and selfish, unwilling to let him live his own life.'

'Maybe so,' she smiled, 'but he was able to stand up to you. Now you know he's not a weak man from having everything done for him but a strong one in spite of it. That should make you proud. He couldn't have turned out that way if you hadn't acted like a good father.'

Rafael kissed her hungrily all over her flushed face, driving her to distraction. 'Somehow you are making me feel very good in spite of all the terrible things I have done. I do not deserve to feel this way. I should be punished, not praised.'

'Oh no, my love, you've been punished enough.' Joanna wound her arms around his neck and kissed him. 'I've only just now realised how much you missed Manuel too. I should have known you weren't as cold and indifferent as you pretended. I should have remembered all that *hot blood and Latin passion . . .*'

His shoulders shook and surprising laughter rumbled deep in his throat. 'Was there ever another like you, Joanna? That morning I saw you in the water with the sun dancing in your hair, you spoke of Latin passion with such loathing.' His arms tightened. 'I nearly lost control. You hurled accusations at me and all I wanted to do was give in to that passion. I had not spent the night with Elena, as you so jealously surmised.' He looked down at her flaming face and all his old arrogance was back, but this time desire mingled with pride. 'Will you be my wife? Will you share my life as my equal, my love?'

'Oh, darling!' she whispered, 'more than anything in the world, I want to be yours and have children like Rodrigo.'

'I shall see what I can do to find his parents. They must be desperate if they were forced to abandon him. I am no Cid, Joanna. I am just an ordinary man. Will you stay with me even when I am unbearable?'

She smiled and pressed herself close against his warm lean length, and he held her as if he would never let her go. 'I understand the Cid's armour was tarnished most of the time,' she murmured against his mouth. 'His wife must have had an awful time trying to make it shine!'

His lips devoured hers and for several minutes there was silence in the study before Rafael drew a little away from her, his eyes glazed with emotion. 'It is late, *mi amada*, but I find I am not at all tired.'

Joanna blushed fiercely and her heart began to pound, but she managed to pin an innocent look on her face. 'Would you like me to get you some warm milk?'

He swept her into his arms and carried her up the stairs. 'Warm milk, indeed! I know a better remedy, and it is much more palatable. I shall recommend it for all the rest of our sleepless nights together!'

Harlequin® Plus

A MAGNIFICENT MATADOR

It was a hot summer day in 1914 when a new young matador named Juan Belmonte walked into Seville's *plaza de toros* to face the bull. Little did the crowd who had gathered to watch the spectacle realize they were about to see, for the first time, one of the greatest matadors who ever lived.

The trumpet sounded, and the ceremony began with the colorful entry of the troop of *banderillos,* or matador assistants, and *picadors,* who ride on horseback carrying short spears. Behind them, in skintight silk trousers, a gold-embroidered waistcoat glittering in the sunlight, a great red cape flung over his shoulder, strode Belmonte.

The mayor of the city threw the key to the bullpen into the ring, and the gate was opened. The bull, defiantly tossing his horns, advanced.

Juan Belmonte stepped dangerously close to the animal and held out his cape. The bull charged. Belmonte executed a pass called the *veronica,* gracefully swerving to avoid the deadly horns—but just barely! The crowd roared approval. No man had ever dared to stand so close to the bull before!

Belmonte became an overnight sensation. He was celebrated for his daring new technique of bullfighting: standing as still and as close to the bull as possible, and diverting the charging animal with skillful capework. Emphasizing not death, but danger, Belmonte revolutionized Spain's national sport. Bullfighting was no longer a battle between a man and a bull, but a battle between a man and his courage.